120

BROGAN: PASSING THROUGH

If Brogan had not stopped at a private well for a drink, life would have been much easier. Instead, he got himself mixed up with Cora Wiesnesky, the widow who owned it, her three children and a shell-shocked old soldier who lived with them, 'Last Post'. Their land was wanted by Edmund and his hired gun, Slade, who believed that there was gold on it, and those varmints were determined to force the family to leave. But Brogan had other ideas . . .

BROGAN: PASSING THROUGH

L. D. Tetlow

A Lythway Book

CHIVERS PRESS
BATH

First published in Great Britain 1987
by
Robert Hale Limited
This Large Print edition published by
Chivers Press
by arrangement with
Robert Hale Limited
1990

ISBN 0 7451 1133 5

British Library Cataloguing in Publication Data

Tetlow, L. D.
  Brogan: passing through.
  I. Title
  823'.914 [F]

  ISBN 0–7451–1133–5

To my agent in acknowledgement for all the hard work and little reward.

CHAPTER ONE

'Hold it right there Mister, move one muscle an' you're a dead man. I mean it.'

Brogan McNally held it right where he was. The voice sounded rather young, but he had no desire to test the ability of its owner to pull the trigger.

'This some trick Edmund's pullin'?' demanded an older voice.

'Trick? Edmund?' asked Brogan, still bent over the well with a ladle of water hovering by his mouth. He had been going to enjoy that water, clean and fresh, a welcome change from the tepid stuff he had been drinking for the past two weeks.

'Don't give us no bullshit,' said the younger voice. 'We heard Edmund was gettin' himself some more hired guns.'

'Can I straighten up?' asked Brogan. 'My back aches enough after ridin' in the saddle all day.'

'Drop your gun Mister,' ordered the young voice. 'Real slow.'

Brogan replaced the ladle back in the well bucket and slowly eased his gun out between his thumb and forefinger, held it out at arms' length and dropped it. 'Now can I straighten up?' The voices grunted, which he took to

1

mean 'yes'. In an act of defiance, he did not turn round straight away, but took the ladle again and had a long slow drink of the cool liquid. Replacing the ladle, he slowly turned to look into the barrel of an ancient buffalo rifle, held by an equally ancient, weather-beaten scrawny man. The rifle may have been ancient, but at the two yards it was away from him, he knew that it was more than capable of blasting him in half.

A little further away stood a boy, he guessed about fifteen, holding a more modern Winchester, aimed unerringly at his chest. The old man seemed to have difficulty keeping the heavy buffalo gun up, the gun wavering between Brogan's chest and legs. Eventually it became too much for the old man to hold up, and he lowered it to the ground, much to Brogan's relief. He had been convinced that the unsteady grip would squeeze the trigger. The boy however, held the Winchester steadily at his chest.

'What's this about "tricks" an' "Edmund"?' asked Brogan.

'Bullshit,' replied the boy. 'You know darned well.'

'If I knew, I wouldn't be askin',' said Brogan. 'Put that thing down boy, it could go off.'

'An' it will,' said the boy. 'If you make any sudden move.'

'Clem's right Mister.' A woman appeared from behind a rock. 'He may be only a boy, but he's quite capable of squeezin' that trigger.'

Brogan did not doubt the accuracy of her words. 'Ma'am, tell him to put that thing down, they're bad enough in the hands of someone who knows how to use 'em, let alone some boy.'

'He knows how to use it Mister,' said the woman. 'Learned almost before he could walk. Okay Mister, explain. If you ain't with Edmund, who the hell are you, an' what you doin' here?'

'I ain't with this Edmund, whoever he is,' said Brogan. 'I'm just a drifter passin' through.'

'Must admit, you don't look like one of Edmund's men,' said the woman. 'I can usually tell 'em a mile off, but we heard he was hirin' guns.'

'I ain't for hire, Ma'am,' assured Brogan. 'I'm just a saddle bum.'

'Okay Clem,' said the woman. 'I believe him. Don't reckon there's any of Edmund's men would have the guts to try anythin' alone.'

The boy reluctantly lowered his rifle and Brogan breathed a little easier. The woman seemed to be good looking, about forty years old, at least he reasoned she would be good looking if her tangle of black hair were straightened up, her rather shabby dress changed and the grime washed off her face.

'You ain't from these parts,' said the woman.

3

'I can tell that, but that don't mean nothin', folks is comin' in all the time.'

'No Ma'am,' said Brogan. 'An' I don't know nothin' 'bout this Edmund feller either, an' I ain't sure I care. You wanna tell this old fool he's too old to play with buffalo rifles, he's liable to kill himself as well.'

'Keep tellin' him not to use the thing,' she said. 'But he won't listen none. Thinks he's back huntin' buffalo.'

'Your father?' asked Brogan, she shook her head. 'Not your husband?'

'Hell no. My man's been gone these past three years,' replied the woman. 'Don't know who the old fool is really. I call him "Last Post" on account of he will insist on playin' his bugle at sunset every night. The kids call him "Gramps", he likes that.'

'Dead?' asked Brogan. 'Your man I mean.'

'Naw ... Just slung his hook one day. Didn't bother me none though, he was useless when he was here, either sleepin' or drunk, usually both.'

Brogan returned to the well and scooped up another ladle of water. 'Best water I had in weeks,' he wiped his sleeve across his mouth.

'Last Post' had found strength to raise the buffalo rifle again and waving it in the general direction of Brogan's stomach. 'Edmund sent you didn't he?' quavered the old man.

Brogan leapt forward, knocking the heavy

4

gun out of the old man's grasp and at the same time sending him crashing to the ground. 'Nobody sent me, I'm my own man, nobody sends me anywhere, an' I don't like anybody pointin' guns at me, especially old dodderers with buffalo guns.'

'Take no heed of the old fool,' said the woman. 'My name's Cora, Cora Wiesnesky. Everyone just calls me Cora. My boy, Clem, you already met. There's two girls in the house, Janie, she's thirteen an' Emily, she's nine.'

'Why so bothered about this Edmund feller?' asked Brogan.

'Wants this land by fair means or foul, an' since fair means ain't workin', he's trying foul,' said Cora.

Brogan looked around. Apart from a few strips of cultivated green a little further down the slope, it seemed a pretty barren place, a bit of moorland grass higher up, but mainly grey and brown dusty rock. 'What's so important about this place? Can hardly imagine why anyone would want to live here, much less fight over it.'

'Gold an' water,' explained Cora. 'Only water for thirty miles in any direction. Even in driest years there's always water. We had a spell of three years once without rain, but there was still plenty water here.'

'Gold?' asked Brogan.

'Yeh, Edmund's got it fixed in his mind

there's gold here too. Sure, we found some in the early days, that's how come I'm here. But there ain't none now. Can't convince Edmund of that though. I own two thousand acres. Two thousand acres of dust, scrub an' rock.'

'Somethin' must've made him think there's gold here.'

'"Last Post",' said Cora. 'Old fool took some gold into town about three months ago. Don't know where the hell he got the stuff from, sure as hell ain't much round here. I know, I looked under almost every rock. Edmund found out, put two an' two together. Only trouble is it don't add up to four.'

'Won't 'Last Post' say where he got the stuff from?'

'No, he just clams up,' said Cora. 'Personally I reckon he found the odd nugget over the years, finally decided to sell 'em in town. We find the odd nugget from time to time, maybe twice a year, but what there is wouldn't pay for one week's diggin'.'

'Okay,' said Brogan. 'So there ain't no gold. So why not just sell up to Edmund? The land looks pretty useless. There sure must be plenty better places to live.'

'Guess I'm just a stubborn old woman,' smiled Cora. 'I like it here. I been here almost twenty years now. I like livin' in the wilds, can't stand towns.'

'Sure, know what you mean,' said Brogan. 'I

6

been driftin' all my life, since I was a kid anyhow. Can't stand towns either.'

'Matter of principle more'n anythin',' said Cora. 'I ain't gonna be pressured by no man. You eaten? I got somethin' on the stove; not much, rabbit stew.'

'Sounds good to me,' said Brogan following Cora round the rocky outcrop, closely followed by a muttering 'Last Post' and a scowling boy. The other two children, Janie and Emily, met them at the door.

'This is Janie,' introduced Cora. 'An' this is Emily. You didn't say what your name was.'

'Brogan, Brogan McNally, but just call me Brogan.'

'What the hell kinda name is Brogan?' laughed Cora.

'I didn't choose it Ma'am,' smiled Brogan.

'No, I guess none of us do,' laughed Cora again.

'You a gunfighter Mister?' asked the youngest, Emily.

'Gunfighter?' said Brogan. 'Hell no. But I can use one if I have to. I guess I can outdraw an' outshoot most men.'

'Bet you can't outdraw Joe Slade,' said Clem.

'Wouldn't know 'bout that,' said Brogan. 'Don't know no Joe Slade.'

'Meanest an' fastest gun in these parts,' said Clem. 'Ain't no man ever beaten him yet. He works for Edmund.'

'Enough of that stupid talk,' scolded Cora. 'Go wash your hands an' face before supper. At once, do you hear?'

The children trooped off, protesting mildly as children do.

'Fine kids Ma'am,' said Brogan. 'Maybe they'd be better off livin' somewheres else. Can't be much fun for 'em here.'

'When they is old enough, they can choose for themselves.'

'Can't be much for you either, no man, 'ceptin' "Last Post". Lots of hard work for a woman.'

'I can do anythin' a man can do,' pouted Cora. 'An' as far as the other thing goes, I gave that up years ago. Finally found out what caused the kids to come along.' She laughed loudly. 'Sure, I miss a man now an' then, but I ain't bothered. You ever had your own woman?'

'No Ma'am,' smiled Brogan. 'Kinda life I lead don't leave much room for a woman. Oh, I been with a couple of women, but I didn't reckon that much to it. Probably it was the women though, whores. I ain't bothered since.'

'Then I'm safe?' laughed Cora.

'Sure thing Ma'am,' assured Brogan naively. Cora seemed somewhat disappointed.

As the children came back Cora told Janie, the eldest girl, to set up the table, then she went off to have a wash herself. Brogan had swilled his face and hands in the well. The homestead was good and solid, built almost entirely of stone, with mud filling. There appeared to be two rooms other than the main room, that alone was unusual, most had only one room. There were two curtained off bunks set in opposite walls, one appeared to be where 'Last Post' slept, as he was sat on it, talking to himself; he assumed the boy, Clem, used the other.

Eventually Cora came back, her hair brushed, a pretty clean dress on, her hands and face washed. She was indeed a very good looking woman. Brogan had the feeling it was all for his benefit, especially when the girls giggled among themselves and glanced coyly at him.

'You weren't plannin' on movin' on tonight were you?' asked Cora. 'We'd like it fine if you stayed here the night.' The girls giggled again and Cora blushed.

The meal had been very good and Brogan sat back contentedly. 'Don't mind if I do. Don't want to put you to no trouble though.'

'Ain't no trouble,' assured Cora, grinning knowingly at him. 'Sorry we ain't got no whisky or beer to offer you.'

'That's okay Ma'am,' said Brogan. 'Never touch the stuff, 'cept maybe a small beer now an' then. My Ma an' Pa put me right off drink.'

'I wish you'd stop callin' me "Ma'am", you make me sound like one of them spinsters what

9

teach in schools ... Just like my man, every cent we ever had went on booze. Ain't had a drop in the house since he left. Wouldn't object to any man likin' a drink now an' then, but I could never stand another drunkard.'

'I got whisky,' giggled 'Last Post'. 'But I ain't sharin' it with no hired gun of Edmund's; it's mine.'

'See what I mean about him?' said Cora. 'Touched in the head. Keeps an old whisky bottle full of water. Just turned up about five years ago, like a fool I felt sorry for him, let him stay.'

'Time to play,' said 'Last Post' looking out of the window. He picked up his bugle and marched stiffly outside.

Brogan was very surprised, the old man played the bugle quite well. 'Old army man I'd guess,' he said. 'He sure knows how to play that thing.'

'My guess too,' agreed Cora. 'Never talks about himself though, 'cept huntin' buffalo. Goes out into the hills with that cannon of his an' its stand; we hear him let off a couple of rounds, then he comes sayin' he killed so many buffalo. Been a long time since there was any buffalo round here.'

Shortly after dark Cora ushered the two younger children off to bed. It seemed they slept in one of the other rooms. The main room was Cora's.

10

'Fine house you got here,' said Brogan, stretching out in front of the fire.

'Only good thing my man ever did,' said Cora. 'That was his trade, buildin', when he was sober enough. Helped build most the town.'

'What town?' asked Brogan. 'Thought you said there was no water for thirty miles.'

'So there ain't,' assured Cora. 'Maneheim is just over thirty miles away, got a river close by. It ain't much now, but it was once, when there was plenty of gold about.'

'Reckon I'll have to go there, I need some supplies.'

'Don't think I can help you much there,' admitted Cora. 'I'm gettin' kinda low myself, 'sides we grow most of our own food.'

'Guess I'll go bed my horse down for the night,' said Brogan. ''Bout time I was turnin' in too.'

He found what Cora called the 'barn' at the back of the house, nothing more than a large shed with two horses and a cow already in it. With his horse, there was not a lot of room left. He looked round for somewhere he could bed down.

'You ain't thinkin' of sleepin' in here are you?' Cora asked from the doorway. 'What's wrong with the house?'

'Don't want to be no trouble,' said Brogan, not really too keen on being lured into the

11

house.

'Told you before, ain't no trouble,' smiled Cora.

'Reckon I could bed down on the floor,' admitted Brogan.

'A bed's more comfortable,' smiled Cora.

'Hell Cora. I ain't slept in a proper bed for years. Don't reckon I could get much sleep in one of them things.'

'So what?' she said sidling up to him.

'Hell Ma'am,' choked Brogan. 'You don't want me. I smell, I ain't had a bath in six months.'

'You can't be any worse than he was,' sniggered Cora.

'Let him stink out here.' Clem stood in the doorway glaring at them, the light of the lamp casting dark shadows across his angry face. 'We don't want no dirty saddle tramp sleepin' in the house.'

'Clem,' snorted Cora. 'You may be the man of the house, but you is still young enough to have your ass tanned. If I want Mister McNally to sleep in the house, it ain't no concern of yours.'

'Janie reckons you only put that dress on so's you could 'tice him,' sulked Clem. 'Guess she was right.'

'Get outa here Clem Wiesnesky, before I throw you out.'

'I'm goin',' pouted Clem. 'Just make sure he

don't sleep in the livin' room. I guess you got a right to let him sleep with you, but I don't like it.'

'Who said anythin' about sleepin' with me?' demanded Cora. 'An' you're right, I can if I want to. Ain't nothin' to do with you.'

Clem vanished into the night and Cora and Brogan looked at each other for a time.

'He was right of course,' said Cora sheepishly. 'I did put on this dress for your benefit. I'm sorry. I guess I was being silly. It's just that I like you an' I ain't had a man since that goodfornothin' left. Don't get many men up here. I don't count "Last Post", could never do nothin' with him, he's too old an' stupid.'

'Might be best if I slept in the barn,' said Brogan. 'You're a mighty fine lookin' woman, an' it's been a long time for me too, but I ain't one to come between a family. Maybe the boy'll calm down. Anyhow, I'll be on my way in the mornin', ain't no sense in gettin' involved.'

Cora's eyes studied the straw on the floor. 'Guess not. Sure, I was bein' stupid. I hardly know you an' you hardly know me. You're right, maybe it is better this way.' As she turned, Brogan caught a glimpse of a tear down her face.

He stood thoughtfully for a few moments, before finally selecting a bed alongside his horse. Even sleeping under the roof of a barn was something that did not happen very often.

13

From the house he heard the raised voices of Clem and his mother, but eventually all was quiet.

He did notice however, that Cora had opened the window to her room.

CHAPTER TWO

Brogan was ready to move before the others were awake and quietly led his horse well away before mounting. The morning was clear and cool and he regretted that he had not even had a cup of coffee to warm him up, but he decided that it might be better all round if he went quickly and quietly.

He had been riding for almost an hour when the sound of several horses made him pull up behind a rock and wait for them to pass. He had no desire to tangle with anyone, friendly or not.

In fact, the four men who rode slowly past looked decidedly unfriendly. He let them pass and sat thoughtfully for a moment. The only reason they would be travelling this way must be to pay a visit on Cora Wiesnesky. Edmund's men. A woman, an old man and a boy would not be much trouble for the likes of men like those.

'What the hell,' he muttered to himself. 'Ain't your fight. Mind your own business

Brogan.' He continued his journey southward, but suddenly found himself turning his horse and heading back in the direction he had come from.

'Told you Brogan McNally, ain't your fight.'

'Go to hell. Can't leave a fine woman like her, or any other woman, to men like that.'

Brogan spent many long hours having conversations with himself and his horse. Sometimes he thought he got more sense out of the horse.

He could be wrong of course, he reasoned; it was just possible that these men were nothing to do with Edmund and were simply passing through. Even so, they looked mean enough to take advantage of a lone woman and children.

He caught a brief glimpse of them up ahead and held back. They did not appear to be in any great hurry, obviously enjoying a joke among themselves. A further glimpse convinced him that these were not travellers, they did not carry the usual trappings of bedrolls and cooking utensils, only guns and water bottles.

The men were obviously not too bothered about being seen, perhaps they had not heard of 'Last Post' and his buffalo gun. That gun could certainly take out one of the riders and probably the horse as well, but it was a muzzle loader and needed time to prime and reload. One shot was all that 'Last Post' would get. The boy could hold out for a time, but not for long against three or four men.

As luck would have it 'Last Post' was not to be seen, nor was Clem. Brogan looked down on the four men approaching the homestead. If Cora heard the men approaching, she made no attempt to hide, standing defiantly with her hands on her hips when she did see them. Brogan eased himself closer.

'Hi there Cora,' grinned one of the men. 'Mister Edmund wants to know if you is gonna accept his last offer. Says it's a very fair one. Five hundred dollars. I got the five hundred with me, an' a paper for you to make your mark on, that makes it legal.'

'I don't have to make no mark,' said Cora. 'Not like you, I can read an' write an' you can tell Edmund that the only mark he's gonna get on his piece of paper is off my ass.'

'Now that ain't friendly Cora,' said the man. 'Mister Edmund is tryin' his best to be friendly. He don't like it when folk ain't friendly with him.'

'Go shit Jim Patterson,' spat Cora. 'I already told him that there ain't no gold on this land, can't he get that into his thick head?'

'Mister Edmund would like to believe you Cora,' said Patterson. 'What he don't understand is why you're so hellfire bent on stoppin'. That makes him kinda suspicious. He thinks that maybe you're holdin' out on him.'

'He can think what he likes, I ain't sellin'.

16

Only way you'll get me off this land is in a pine box. Now get goin' back to your master like the frightened cur you are.'

Patterson's face tightened up in anger. 'We had our orders Cora. We was told that either we went back with paper signed or we was to settle it any way we decided. Looks like we got no choice.'

'First though,' grinned one of the others. 'We give you a taste of what you been missin' since your old man took off. You got two daughters too, pity if they was to die not knowing what a man was like.'

'You leave my girls outa this,' screamed Cora. 'Me you can do anythin' you like with, but touch those girls an' I'll kill you.'

'You'll be dead by then,' grinned Patterson, about to get off his horse.

'An' you'll be dead before your feet reach the ground,' barked Brogan behind them.

Patterson froze, but one of the other men swung round, only to receive a blast from Brogan's rifle which sent him sprawling lifeless in the dust.

'So, the little lady's got herself some help,' hissed Patterson looking down at his lifeless companion. 'You just made a big mistake Mister.'

'Seems like your friend made the mistake,' grunted Brogan. 'Now, drop your guns, rifles too, slow, or you end up like him.'

17

They did as they were ordered and Brogan moved in front of them.

'Okay Cora,' sneered Patterson. 'Your friend's got the drop on us now, but we can wait. Don't know who you are Mister, but from now on your days are numbered; you're a dead man.'

'Not yet,' said Brogan. 'Now pick him up an' get the hell outa here while you still can. I ain't fussy, I'll drop you where you are.'

Patterson nodded to the others who pushed the body over the saddle, one of them then going to pick up their weapons.

'They stay,' ordered Brogan. 'Just in case you got plans.'

'You'd send a man out there with no gun?' asked Patterson.

'Seems to me the only ones who got nothin' to fear is you,' said Brogan.

'Mister,' said Patterson. 'I'd ride out now while you still got some sorta chance. Mister Edmund don't like folk interferin' in his business.'

'An' I don't like folk what threaten women an' kids,' said Brogan. 'But I guess that's all the guts you got.'

Patterson grunted and turned his horse round and rode off, followed by the other two leading the dead man's horse. Brogan ran up a small hill to make sure they were well on their way.

'Thanks Brogan,' said Cora when he walked

18

back to the house carrying the guns. 'But I don't think you helped none.'

'They was goin' to kill you,' gasped Brogan. 'An' the kids.'

'Clem had 'em covered,' pointed Cora. Clem appeared at the door with his rifle, not looking too pleased.

'Yea,' snarled Clem. 'I could've handled 'em. Didn't need no help from no saddle tramp.'

'I reckon you only made matters worse,' sighed Cora.

'If that's all the thanks I get, maybe I should've listened to myself. I will next time.'

'Brogan,' said Cora. 'I really am grateful, ain't many men would've bothered, an' if you want you can stick around, that would help. I know you did what you thought best, it's just that Edmund ain't gonna like it. He'll be even more determined now.'

'We don't need him,' snapped Clem. 'They threatened Ma before, but I made 'em run.'

'They ever threaten the girls before?' asked Brogan.

'No,' admitted Cora. 'That's the first time, but I reckon it was just talk. Don't reckon even Edmund would stoop that low.'

'I ain't so sure,' said Brogan. 'I reckon they mean it.'

'Yeh, maybe,' sighed Cora.

'Take their advice Mister,' said Clem. 'Clear out now while you got a chance. We don't need

19

you round here.'

'Clem's right,' said Cora. 'You stoppin's only gonna make matters worse.'

'Okay,' said Brogan. 'I can take a hint. From now on you're on your own. You can fight your own battles. I don't wanna know no more. Sorry I spoiled the party.'

Without another word he threw the armful of guns onto the ground and mounted his horse. Cora watched, tears in her eyes, as he disappeared down the valley.

*　　　*　　　*

'Four of you let one lousy saddle tramp take you?' demanded Phil Edmund. 'You're supposed to be gunfighters, an' now I got me one gun less. Maybe I should hire this bum an' get rid of you.'

'We didn't know he was there Mister Edmund,' wailed Patterson. 'He just appeared from nowhere.'

'Magician too is he?' scorned Edmund from behind his large highly-polished desk.

'He wasn't there yesterday,' said one of the other men. 'I watched the place from ten in the mornin' till after two.'

'Well he's there now,' said Edmund. 'Wonder you didn't let that old fool "Last Post", or whatever they call him, take you out.'

'He was out in the hills shootin' at pretend

buffalo,' grinned the other man.

'Maybe you should join him, that's about all you're good for.'

'I ain't gonna let this saddle tramp get away with it,' snarled Patterson. 'No man takes me on an' lives.'

''Ceptin' maybe Joe Slade,' said Edmund.

'Him too,' said Patterson. 'Just as well we're on the same side.'

'I don't reckon that saddle bum's gonna stay around,' said Edmund. Types like him don't. Must admit though, he seems different; most would have wanted nothin' to do with it.'

'I sent Karl Evans back to keep an eye on things,' said Patterson. 'If he moves, I'll soon know. Then we can deal with Wiesnesky woman an' all the rest of 'em.'

''Cept "Last Post",' warned Edmund. 'I need him to show me where the gold is.'

'Don't worry Mister Edmund,' answered Patterson. 'We don't harm him none.'

'I do worry,' sighed Edmund. ''Specially after this.'

'Won't happen again,' said Patterson. 'We'll be ready for him next time.'

'You'd better be,' said Edmund. ''Cos next time it might be just you that gets killed.'

'Saddle bums ain't gunfighters,' smiled Patterson. 'He got lucky, that's all.'

Edmund waved his hand to dismiss them and returned to his papers.

21

'What about the woman?' asked Patterson at the door.

'Maybe I'd better send out a couple of cripples,' sneered Edmund. 'They couldn't do no worse than you. Forget her for the moment. I'll tell you when.'

An hour later Karl Evans returned with the news that Brogan was heading toward town.

★   ★   ★

Brogan was in no hurry and his horse was grateful for that. It was late afternoon when he came upon the town of Maneheim sprawling below him. His first reaction was to avoid the place, but he needed supplies and reluctantly decided to ride in.

The town had obviously seen better days, there appeared to be more derelict buildings than those in use. Maneheim boasted a general store, a saloon with no name and a run-down livery stable. There was no sign of a Sheriff's Office, for which he was most grateful. Brogan and sheriffs rarely saw eye-to-eye.

'Five pounds of beans, a bag of salt an' a bag of flour,' said Brogan to the storekeeper. He wandered about looking at what else there was as the man made up the order. He took a small side of smoke dried bacon off the shelf and dropped it along with the others.

'Three fifty,' said the storekeeper. 'Just

22

passin' through?' Brogan nodded. 'They all pass through since the gold ran out.'

'I hear some still think there's gold about.'

'Hummph!' grunted the storekeeper. 'Edmund you mean. Sure there's gold about, but Edmund owns the only mines still got gold. Rest of 'em ran out years ago. Edmund owns them too. Old nugget turns up now an' then, but nothin' to cause a gold rush over. 'Sides, Edmund's got it sewn up pretty tight.'

'No sheriff either,' observed Brogan.

'No need,' replied the storekeeper. 'We had one for a while, when the gold fever was at its height, but he got killed. We ain't bothered since.'

Brogan paid his bill and loaded his purchases onto his horse and led it further along the street to a water trough. The sight of the horse drinking reminded him he was thirsty. He decided that one of his very infrequent beers was in order.

The saloon was small, dark and dirty, but the beer was remarkably good. There were four other customers, two very worn out looking bar girls and the fat bartender. One of the girls sidled over to him and slipped her arm through his.

'Buy a girl a drink?' she asked trying to look attractive through the layers of thick make-up. Brogan detested too much make-up on a woman, but realised that without make-up her

23

face might fall off.

'Beat it,' he grunted.

'For two dollars,' the girl tried to smile through her bright red lips. 'I can show you a good time.'

'Wouldn't pay two cents for a tramp like you,' snarled Brogan. 'Beat it I said.'

The girl pouted. 'Maybe you prefer Fat Pete here. I heard of men like you.'

'Lady,' sighed Brogan, 'I like a woman just as much as the next man, but I'm particular. A dose of pox is somethin' I can live without.'

'You accusin' me of bein' dirty?' shouted the girl. 'More likely I'll catch somethin' off you. Anyhow, you stink.'

'Surprised you noticed. You ain't no fresh flower yourself.'

The girl stormed off to rejoin her companion, glaring hatred at him.

'That's Joe Slade's girl,' said Fat Pete.

'Then Joe Slade can't be too particular,' replied Brogan.

'Ain't nobody can be too particular in these parts,' said Fat Pete. 'Apart from a few settlers' wives, them's all we got.'

'Reckon I'd prefer some tired old wife,' said Brogan. 'I heard about this Joe Slade. He a big man round here?'

'Naw, not really,' said Fat Pete. 'He works for Edmund, hired gun.'

'I heard of him too,' said Brogan. 'Seems he

owns most of the territory. 'What he want hired guns for?'

'Got himself some kinda war goin' with Jed Balsam, over in Seely Flats. Sold what he thought was a worn-out mine to Balsam, only Balsam struck it rich. Now Edmund wants the mine back again.'

'Maybe he should stick to that 'stead of tryin' to run women an' kids off their land.'

'Cora Wiesnesky,' grunted Fat Pete. 'You met her?' Brogan nodded. 'They been at each other's throats for three months now, ever since that old fool "Last Post" brought in that gold. Gold's the only thing Edmund thinks about.'

'This Joe Slade,' said Brogan. 'I hear he's supposed to be pretty handy with a gun.'

'Ain't nobody ever seen anyone better,' assured Fat Pete. 'Don't do to tangle with him. Helen, that's his girl, she'll tell him for sure what you said to her. He won't like that.'

'Tough. Seems he don't mind her whorin' for a livin' though.'

Fat Pete shrugged his shoulders. 'That's how things are.'

Suddenly the saloon door burst open and three men crashed through. Brogan recognised them as the three he had met at Cora's place.

'So,' snarled Patterson. 'You're still here, bum.'

Brogan looked at them distastefully, but he was steeled for action. 'Why not? I ain't got

25

nothin' to worry about.'

The other occupants of the saloon hastily beat a retreat through the door and the girls ran into the back room. Fat Pete moved down the bar out of the line of fire.

'You shouldn't have interfered,' snapped Patterson. 'No concern of yours.'

'I ain't interferin' now,' smiled Brogan.

'Once is enough,' said Patterson. 'You killed our buddy, we don't like that. Mister Edmund don't like it either.'

'Tough shit on you an' Edmund,' said Brogan.

'Brave talk for a saddle bum,' grinned Patterson. 'But you ain't got the drop on us now. I hope you made your will Mister, 'cos if you ain't it's too late now.'

'You want revenge,' smiled Brogan. 'Let's see if you're as fast with your gun as you are with your mouth.'

'I'm good Mister,' snarled Patterson. 'Only one man better'n me.'

'Don't tell me,' said Brogan. 'Joe Slade.'

'That's right, an' I reckon I could take him too if I had to.'

'Big talk from a man that needs three others to take one woman an' three kids. I see it needs three of you to take me as well.'

'You can say what you like,' sneered Patterson. 'Sure I like the odds well in my favour, only fools go it alone.'

26

'Then why ain't you alone?' goaded Brogan. Dying was something that Brogan had never worried about; he knew his time would come, probably at the receiving end of a bullet, but it did not bother him.

The three men moved, but Brogan was ready. In an instant his gun was in his hand barking its message at one of the men who slumped wide-eyed to the floor. At the same time he threw himself rolling onto the floor. A bullet singed past his ear and his gun spat twice more. Another groan and thud onto the wooden floor and Brogan was up on his knees.

Patterson slowly let his gun slip from his fingers as he clutched his shoulder, looking more than a little surprised. Brogan was up kicking their guns away. Patterson still seemed unable to believe that he had been hit. The two men on the floor seemed to be still alive, groaning painfully.

'Okay,' grinned Brogan. 'Seems your luck is still with you. Get these two outa here an' tell this Edmund that if he sends anyone else after me, he'll have nobody left to fight Balsam with, an' make sure he leaves Cora Wiesnesky alone.'

Fat Pete helped the wounded men onto their horses and watched with a certain amount of satisfaction as they rode slowly away. 'Nice shootin',' he said to Brogan as he came back. 'Ain't seen fancy shootin' like that since I was back in Tucson fifteen years ago.'

'Think so?' said Brogan. 'Bloody awful. They should've been dead. Guess I'm short on practice.'

'Edmund ain't gonna like it,' observed Fat Pete. 'No sir, he ain't gonna like it at all. Take my advice Mister, move on now while you can. He's sure to send Joe Slade after you. Even if he don't, Slade'll come anyhow. Don't like to think there's a gun around faster than he is. Kinda takes pride in it.'

'Tough on Joe Slade,' said Brogan.

'Them three wasn't no slouches either,' continued Fat Pete. 'Patterson's reckoned to be almost as good as Slade.'

'Then I ain't got nothin' to worry about,' grinned Brogan.

'In a straight draw, I guess not,' agreed Fat Pete. 'But don't count on Slade playin' fair. He plays mean an' dirty.'

'I can play dirty too,' said Brogan. 'I've had to, to stay alive sometimes.'

The shooting had attracted the residents of Maneheim, and they now all came trooping into the saloon to stand and stare at the stranger who had taken out three of Edmund's best men.

'I give him until tomorrow if he stops round,' said one to the man at his side.

'I reckon I'm goin' fishin' tomorrow,' came the reply. 'There's liable to be a few stray bullets flyin' around, I don't aim to stop one of 'em.'

28

'Think I'll join you,' said the first man.

At least Fat Pete was pleased, since they were in the saloon, most decided that they might as well have a drink. He pushed a glass of beer at Brogan. 'On the house,' he grinned. 'Ain't had this much trade this early in the day for years, thanks to you.'

'Glad to be of service,' grinned Brogan taking the beer.

As it was too late to travel far, Brogan decided that he had better find somewhere to stay the night. As there was no shortage of empty buildings, he wandered off to find one that was not quite so derelict as the others. He eventually found one which had a weather-beaten sign outside proclaiming it had belonged to one 'Doc Grant M.D.'

At the back of the house was a large patch of long green grass which he turned his horse onto and humped his saddle into the house. In one of the downstairs rooms he found a bed complete with dusty mattress and in another, the kitchen, a stove and water pump. After a few pushes of the pump handle, a gurgle of muddy water appeared, and after a few more the water turned clear.

Outside was a water barrel which his horse had found. 'All the luxury you could want,' he said to his horse which neighed and shook his head, as it always did when he spoke to it.

Brogan could be very pigheaded when he

wanted to be. He hated being run out of town by bigotted sheriffs and he hated to run from a challenge, even though he knew that one day he would end up dead.

There was no shortage of wood for the fire, and soon his bacon and beans were cooking. He would worry about tomorrow in the morning.

CHAPTER THREE

'So, the saddle tramp ain't no gunfighter,' growled Edmund. 'Well he sure is one hell of a good imitation. Now I got me three cripples on my hands.'

'He ain't no ordinary saddle tramp that's for sure,' wailed Patterson as Edmund's wife dug into the wound. The other two had barely made it back to Edmund's white hacienda-style fortress. They lay almost lifeless in their bunks, hardly breathing at all. Another sharp dig brought a loud cry of pain and a violent twist of his body.

'Lie still and be quiet,' ordered Mrs Edmund. 'What you really need is a doctor, but since there ain't one for a hundred miles, you'll have to put up with me. Now lie still, I've got to get the bullet out unless you want it to go bad ways.'

Patterson tried to relax, Edmund replaced the

strip of wood in Patterson's mouth to stop him biting his tongue. Mrs Edmund gave another hard dig with the kitchen knife she was using and Patterson's back arched in agony, sweat pouring from his forehead. Edmund pushed the tortured body down.

'Got it,' sighed Mrs Edmund wiping her sleeve across her head. 'Went deep, but it's out now.'

Patterson passed out.

'Want me to go after him?' A tall rangy man stood by the bunkhouse door fingering his gun, a cheroot hanging wetly from his lips.

'I want that tramp,' said Edmund. 'But I want him alive; anyhow he may just give you the same treatment he gave them.'

'Maybe,' grunted Slade. 'But I wasn't figurin' on givin' him the chance.'

'Neither did they,' said Edmund.

'Yeh, but now we know he's good with a gun, maybe even as good as me, so I don't aim to try him face to face.'

'In the back,' said Edmund. 'I reckon that's the only way you'll get him. No Joe, I need him alive, an' I need you alive, 'specially now these three are laid up. I hear Balsam's got himself some more guns. I want this stranger on my side an' I intend to have him.'

Slade shrugged. 'You're the boss. Personally I'd rather kill him.'

'Can't stand the thought there's someone

better'n you, can you? Sure, you can go get him, but I want him back here alive. Got that?'

'An' supposin' he won't play ball?' asked Slade.

'Then we persuade him,' replied Edmund.

'Just how you figurin' on doin' that?'

'He'll have a choice. Work for me or die.'

'You could never trust him,' said Slade. 'Them kinda wages don't inspire much confidence.'

'Then we buy him. Man like that has his price, all men do, some just come more expensive than others.'

'An' after we've got rid of Balsam?'

'He's yours to do what the hell you like with.'

'I'd rather kill him first,' said Slade. 'We got more men than Balsam. I say hit Balsam with everythin' we've got.'

'Two, maybe three reasonable men with guns. Rest is rubbish, you know that as well as I do. They'd run as soon as the goin' got rough.'

'Okay,' shrugged Slade again. 'Guess it won't hurt none to try it. But if it don't work, I take him out. Agreed?'

'Agreed,' said Edmund.

Mrs Edmund, a strikingly good looking blonde, had turned her attention to the two men lying in their bunks. 'Gorman's a goner, ain't nothin' I can do for him. Looks like the bullet shot his kidneys to hell.'

Edmund nodded at the other man. 'Be a long time before he's handlin' a gun again. Looks like his arm's busted as well.'

'Fell off his horse on the way back,' said Mrs Edmund. 'Bullet went through his chest, missed the heart an' lungs though. I can feel it just under the skin by his shoulder blade. Soon have that out. He should be okay.' She turned the man over and cut into the flesh. Fortunately for him he was unconscious and did not feel Mrs Edmund's none-too-careful surgery.

* * *

Brogan was suddenly wide awake, his body tensed for action, his ears straining to catch the slightest sound. It was still dark, except for a very slight paling on the horizon, which he could see through the broken window. Something had woken him; what, he had no idea. Now there was nothing to be heard.

Years of sleeping in the open had accustomed him to the natural noises around him, but this time he knew it was something different. Still there was no sound from outside, except the distant gurgle of water rushing noisily along the river. Survival had been the name of Brogan's life and he knew better than dismiss something like this as simply his imagination.

Quickly and quietly he slipped into the cold morning, eyes and ears alert. His old horse too was slightly restless. That convinced him. She was always restless when something was amiss.

*   *   *

Joe Slade and six other men burst in on Fat Pete, one of them clamping his hand across Fat Pete's mouth to stop him from crying out. Fat Pete gazed wide eyed with horror at the dark shadows above him.

'Not a sound you fat slob,' whispered Slade. 'Where's this saddle tramp holin' up?'

The man with his hand over Fat Pete's mouth slowly eased his hand away. The cold round end of a gun at his temple persuaded Fat Pete not to cry out.

'You heard me,' whispered Slade again. 'Where is he?'

Fat Pete broke out into a sweat and gulped. 'Doc Grant's old house.'

'You sure?'

'Sure I'm sure,' gulped Fat Pete again. 'I saw him in there, beddin' down.'

'Lot of help you were when he took them three.'

'You know me,' gasped Fat Pete. 'I don't take sides.'

''Cos you're yeller through an' through,' sneered Slade.

'If you say so Mister Slade,' sweated Fat Pete.

34

'I say so,' hissed Slade. 'Okay, you'd better be right. 'Cos if you ain't we'll come back an' get you. That's a promise.'

'He's there okay Mister Slade,' gulped Fat Pete. 'Why should I lie to you?'

'Go back to sleep you fat slob,' warned Slade. 'Don't you dare show your face. Got that?'

'Got it Mister Slade.' Fat Pete had every intention of staying exactly where he was.

'Let's go,' instructed Slade. 'Be quiet an' remember, Mister Edmund wants this bum alive.'

The men slid quietly out of the room and Fat Pete pulled the blankets over his head and shivered.

Slade sent four men round the back of the house while he led the other two stealthily to the front. He flattened himself against the wall and slowly looked through the broken window. At first he could see nothing, but slowly he began to make out the bed and the saddle on the floor. The room was empty and he considered bursting through the front door, but decided it was too risky, he had no liking for being on the receiving end of a gun shot. He motioned the two with him to take cover and keep the front of the house covered.

Slipping quietly round the back, he found one of the other men crouched behind the water butt. The man nodded toward the now very restless horse. Slade seemed satisfied. The back

35

door was hanging on its hinges and Slade eased himself through and into the kitchen.

It had become lighter now as dawn began to break, and he could make out the cooking utensils still on the stove. The rest of the house was silent. He waved one of the men to follow him. The others kept out of sight. A search of the house proved it to be empty.

'Damn,' muttered Slade. 'Where the hell is he?'

'Ain't far, that's for sure,' said the other man, Karl Evans. 'His saddle an' horse are still here.'

Slade smiled to himself. 'I'll say this for him, he sure ain't no ordinary drifter. He's good. I'm gonna enjoy catchin' him, then later I'm gonna enjoy killin' him. Don't reckon there's much point in lookin' for him, he could be anywhere. He's got his rifle with him, we'd be sittin' ducks.'

'Do we take his saddle an' horse?' asked Evans.

'No wouldn't do no good,' said Slade. 'Karl, you an' Slim head south, lie up somewhere in case he comes your way. Jack an' Frank can lie up north. If he leaves town one of you head back to me, I'll be back at the house. Don't do nothin', just keep him in your sights.'

The men dispersed to their allotted tasks. Slade marched down the street. 'Okay wise guy,' he shouted. 'You win this time, but Mister Edmund wants to see you. If I were you

36

I'd accept his invitation.' As he expected, there was no reply.

Fat Pete gazed up for the second time at a gun pointed at his head. 'I had to tell 'em Mister,' he wailed. 'They'd've killed me else. I don't take sides. Don't pay. Slade's a mean one.'

'So am I,' hissed Brogan. He eased the gun back into its holster, much to the relief of Fat Pete. 'Okay, I can understand you don't want to get involved. I heard Slade call out that this Edmund wanted to see me. Know anythin'?'

'No sir,' assured Fat Pete, ''cept that if Mister Edmund wants somethin', he gets it.'

'Seems you was wrong when you said Slade would want to kill me.'

'He wants to kill you all right,' said Fat Pete. 'But I heard him say that Edmund wanted you alive. I guess he wants to make a deal.'

'I don't deal with nobody,' said Brogan. 'If he thinks I'm for sale, he's mistaken.'

'Yes sir, whatever you say.'

'You tell him that,' said Brogan. 'His men are sure to be in town later lookin' for me. Tell him I ain't for sale.'

'Yes sir,' assured Fat Pete. 'But it don't do to cross Mister Edmund.'

Brogan snorted and left Fat Pete to sweat. The sky was now bright and the first stirrings of life could be seen in Maneheim. Slade and his men were nowhere to be seen. Brogan decided to forget about his breakfast.

*　　*　　*

'Can't say I'm surprised,' said Edmund. 'I guessed this feller warn't no ordinary drifter. But I still want him.'

'I left men posted out of town in case he leaves, we'll know which way he's headed. He won't be able to make much time on that tired old horse of his.'

'Alive remember,' said Edmund. 'He ain't no use to me dead.'

'Sounds interestin', this saddle tramp,' smiled Mrs Edmund. 'Makes a change from the usual trash around here.'

'Keep your interest to yourself,' said Edmund. 'This is purely business. I don't want you makin' eyes at him.'

'You didn't say that when you wanted me to get to Balsam,' smiled Mrs Edmund. 'You'd've let him take me to bed.'

'That was different,' snarled Edmund. 'An' remember this Amy, I took you out of the gutter to give you what you got now. You do as I say. If I say you go to bed with Balsam, you go, just like I say keep your eyes off this saddle tramp, unless you wanna end up back in the whorehouse.'

'Don't worry,' laughed Amy. 'I don't intend to give this up too easily. I married you for your

38

money, not because I loved you. I get the lifestyle I want, you get what you want from me. It's as good an arrangement as any. Mercenary, but good.'

'Bitch,' snarled Edmund. 'But I guess you're right.'

'How's Jim an' the others?' asked Slade.

'Gorman died just after you left,' said Amy. 'Idaho, he'll be okay in a few weeks. Jim's sore, but he'll be fine. Won't be much use with a gun for a while though.'

'He'll just have to rely on his big mouth,' laughed Slade.

'I hope you don't have to rely on yours,' said Edmund. 'You reckon you'll be able to take this drifter?'

'I reckon so,' answered Slade. 'I got one advantage he ain't got. I know this country.'

'He sounds obstinate,' said Amy. 'Maybe he don't want to know. Maybe it'd be better if you just forgot him.'

'You know me Amy,' said Edmund. 'When I've made my mind up there's no stoppin' me. Either this drifter works for me, or he never works again.'

'Sure,' laughed Amy. 'I know you.'

Two hours later the news came that Brogan had left town and was heading back north.

★   ★   ★

Despite his gut feelings, Brogan decided to see if Cora and the children were unharmed. He was greeted by 'Last Post' and the buffalo rifle.

'Put that thing down,' ordered Cora. 'So, you've come back Brogan McNally. What for?'

'Just thought I'd check see if you was still in one piece.'

'An' if I hadn't been?'

Brogan shrugged. 'Dunno really. Maybe give you a decent burial.'

'I don't understand you,' smiled Cora. 'You said yourself you didn't want to know anymore.'

'Reckon I don't understand me either,' replied Brogan. 'I had a visit from that Patterson an' his two cronies yesterday, in the saloon in Maneheim. I reckon at least one of 'em's dead by now. I winged Patterson pretty bad too.'

'Maybe you should've killed 'em while you had the chance.'

'Don't believe in killin' for the sake of it,' smiled Brogan. 'I also had a visit from Joe Slade. Didn't give him no chance to find me. Shouted somethin' about Edmund wantin' to see me.'

'Guess he wants to hire you,' said Cora.

'Reckon so,' agreed Brogan. 'But I ain't for hire.'

'Why don't you work for Edmund?' growled Clem. 'You could do his dirty work an' kill us.

Maybe you is workin' for him now.'

'Son,' sighed Brogan. 'If you ain't careful, when you grow up, if you grow up, you'll be walkin' lopsided.'

'What you talkin' about?' demanded Clem.

'That chip on your shoulder, it's gettin' bigger all the time.'

'That's my business Mister.'

'Whatever you say son,' agreed Brogan. He looked at Cora. 'I sure could use a coffee an' a bite to eat.'

Cora smiled. 'Bastard. Sure, coffee's always on. I got some cheese an' some bread. That'll have to do.'

'Sounds fine,' said Brogan.

Clem stormed off, angry at his mother for allowing Brogan to stay.

'Take no heed of the boy,' sighed Cora. 'He's young an' impatient. Strangely enough he doted on his Pa. Blamed me when he took off. Resents it every time I even talk to another man.'

'Natural a boy should look up to his father,' said Brogan. 'Mind, I hated mine, my Ma too.'

'Guess so,' sighed Cora. 'I'd rather he accepted the truth of what his father really was though, a drunk.'

'He will in time,' assured Brogan.

The girls at least seemed pleased to see him, engaging in their usual habit of nudging and giggling at each other and giving knowing glances at Brogan and their mother. 'Last Post' sat on his bed talking to himself and cleaning the ancient buffalo rifle.

'More cheese?' asked Cora.

'No more thanks,' burped Brogan. 'That was just fine.'

'I left my window open the other night,' said Cora blushing.

'I saw,' said Brogan. 'Believe me, it took all my willpower not to climb through.'

'An' it took all mine not to join you in the barn,' admitted Cora. 'Ever thought of settlin' down?'

'Sure, many times,' said Brogan. 'But I know it wouldn't work. Might be all right for a time, but I'd get the wanderlust an' be on my way again.'

'Well, you gotta make some sort of decision,' said Cora. 'Either you get the hell outa my life right now, or stay. You can't keep runnin' back here every five minutes to see if I'm okay.'

'I know that,' said Brogan. 'An' I reckon this is the last time. I'll be on my way. For your own sakes though, sell up to Edmund. I hate to think of what his boys'll do to you an' the kids.'

Cora looked at him tearfully. 'I guess you're right. But I'd rather make a fight of it with your help.'

'Fine woman like you could sure find a better man than me. One that'll look after you, one that has a bit of money.'

'Maybe so,' said Cora. 'But I don't reckon I want them. I'm too independent. I like my freedom.'

'An' you reckon you'd still be free with me around?'

'In a way, yeh,' replied Cora. 'You an' me, we're two of a kind. Don't like towns, both pigheaded. I wouldn't make no demands on you, an' I don't think you'd make any on me.'

'Naw,' grinned Brogan. 'I get very possessive 'bout some things, reckon you'd be one of 'em. Wouldn't work.'

'Okay then,' choked Cora. 'You'd better go now, before I cry. I hate cryin'. I ain't cried in years.'

'Reckon so,' agreed Brogan. He left Cora staring at the table, tears welling up in her eyes, and rode out, heading west.

*　　　*　　　*

He had the feeling that he was being followed for some time, in fact ever since he had left Cora, but whoever it was was keeping well out of sight. If he was being followed there was only one of them.

'Could be Indians,' he said to himself.

'Don't be stupid. Nearest Indians is thirty or forty miles away, an' they're a pretty peaceable lot.'

'Who then?'

'Edmund. One of Edmund's men.'

'Only one?'

'Maybe there were more. Other's gone off for help.'

'Yeh, probably.'

Brogan, satisfied that he was right, became more alert. The countryside was mainly rock and scrub, the odd twisted thorn tree and a few towering cactus. Ideal country for an ambush. He kept to the high ground as much as possible.

There seemed no other way through. The river bed cut through a canyon some forty or fifty feet wide, with sheer sides up to two hundred feet. He could not see just how far it went as it swung right almost as soon as it started. There was only a trickle of water bouncing its way along the rocky bed, so there was no problem in getting through. However, he had sensed that his companion had disappeared some ten minutes earlier, and this fact worried him a lot more than if he had still been following.

There was another way, but that meant a very precarious looking climb up the steep hillside just before the canyon.

'Pity you ain't a goat or a mule,' he said to his horse, receiving a neigh and a shake of the head in answer. 'No. Right now it might be better if you were. I suppose I could lead you up, but neither of us is gettin' any younger.' Another neigh and a shake of the head. 'Don't like the

44

idea of goin' through that canyon. If they intend to kill us, that'd be the ideal spot. Even if they don't, we'd be boxed in. Sorry old girl, but you gotta do some climbin'.' The horse shook its head and snorted. 'No use sayin' you can't. You got to.'

He jumped out of the saddle and led the horse up the gentler lower slopes to what appeared to be a narrow path, in some places no more than a foot wide, with a steep drop below them. Brogan and his old horse had been together over ten years and a kind of mutual understanding had grown up between them. The horse allowed itself to be led, slowly picking its way up the twisting slope.

For a brief moment Brogan thought he was going to lose his beloved horse as the ledge crumbled and she fought to retain her foothold, but regain it she did.

'Good girl,' encouraged Brogan. 'Not much further now, keep goin'.' Gradually the track levelled off as they neared the top and the going became easier. 'Made it old girl,' he panted. 'Reckon we earned ourselves a rest a bit further up.'

The ground flattened out and then dipped into a hollow. Normally he would have avoided the hollow, but at the bottom, among some rocks, he saw a waterhole. A scan of the surrounding land indicated that all was safe.

'Water old girl,' said Brogan. 'Reckon we

both need some after that climb.'

He led the horse down to the waterhole and was a little surprised that she seemed unwilling. She pawed the ground nervously, refusing to drink. Brogan had his gun in his hand and was about to dive behind a rock when a voice told him to freeze. He froze.

'How'd you know we was here?' demanded Slade. 'We sure as hell never moved a muscle, an' our horses is down the hillside a way.'

'What makes you think I knew?'

'Practisin' your draw was you?'

'Okay, I knew, but I found out a little late. You Joe Slade?'

'Yeh,' came the unseen reply. 'Flattered you heard of me.'

'Oh I heard,' grinned Brogan. 'I heard about how you was only just a little bit better'n Patterson with a gun. How are they by the way, dead I hope?'

'One dead, one pretty badly crippled. That warn't all your doin' though, fell off his horse an' busted his arm. Patterson won't use a gun for a while, but he ain't so bad.'

'Have to use his mouth instead,' laughed Brogan.

'My words exactly,' laughed Slade from the cover of a rock. 'At least we think alike on that.'

'I must be gettin' old,' said Brogan. 'The three of 'em should've been dead, an' I just got myself ambushed. Okay Slade get it over with

46

now, you might as well kill me.'

'No sir,' laughed Slade. 'I would if it was left to me, but Mister Edmund said for me to bring you back alive. Mind he didn't say nothin' about not bein' crippled, but he must've meant that too. Drop your gun Mister.'

'No,' said Brogan defiantly. 'One thing I ain't bothered about is dyin', 'cept I aint got where I'm goin' yet.'

'Where's that?'

'Don't know, ain't never reached there yet. Maybe this is it. Anyhow, how the hell you know I was comin' this way? The man you had followin' me sure couldn't tell you, he left me a couple of miles back.'

'You knew he was there?'

'Sure, picked him up just after I left the Wiesnesky place. Reckon there must've been two of 'em.'

'There was,' came Slade's voice. 'I reckon I got you figured Mister. What is your name?'

'Brogan, just call me Brogan.'

'I got you figured Brogan. I'd probably've done the same as you did. That canyon was a death trap. I figured you just might've spotted your tail, thought what I'd've done an' here we are. Even if you didn't, we could easily have picked you up again.'

'Seems we got somethin' of a Mexican stand off,' said Brogan. 'you want me alive an' in one piece, an' I ain't droppin' the gun.'

47

'Yeh,' agreed Slade. 'I must admit we got a problem. There's six men surroundin' you, but you're right, Edmund wants you in one piece, he wants to hire you.'

'An' I don't want to be hired.'

'Ain't so bad. Money's good, an' Amy Edmund is a bit of a goer.'

'Not interested.'

'Well now,' Slade stood up. 'I reckon I've got the winnin' hand. You see, if you don't at least talk to Edmund, then I got his permission to kill you. I was all in favour of killin' you, but it wouldn't give me no satisfaction no more.'

'Think you can?' grinned Brogan his gun pointing at Slade. For a few moments they studied each other before Slade laughed.

'Hell man, I ain't never met anybody like you. I do believe you're quite willin' to die.'

'At least I'll have the satisfaction of takin' you with me. I can do that, before I get shot in the back.'

'Look Brogan,' smiled Slade. 'I kinda like you. I don't want to kill you. Tell you what. Come with me, talk to Edmund, then if you still say no, you can be on your way. I was goin' to kill you if you refused, but I'll give up that pleasure.'

Brogan decided that at least it would buy him time.

'Okay. I'll talk, but I go in as free man, not as your prisoner.'

'Agreed,' grinned Slade.

CHAPTER FOUR

'So you're the elusive saddle tramp?' Edmund lay back in his leather chair and gazed at Brogan on the other side of his overlarge desk. 'Don't look nothin' special to me.'

'An' you're the famous Mister Edmund I been hearin' so much about. You don't look much to me either,' replied Brogan.

Edmund inclined his head and smiled slightly. 'Touché Mister Brogan. Touché.'

'Just Brogan. Full name's Brogan McNally, but I prefer Brogan.'

'As you wish,' continued Edmund. 'Obviously looks don't mean a thing. In your case you don't look like a gunfighter...'

'I ain't,' interrupted Brogan.

'... An' I don't give you the impression of bein'... What...? A rich man, a hard man?' continued Edmund.

'Rich? yes,' replied Brogan. 'But I seen harder lookin' school Ma'ams.'

'So have I Brogan,' smiled Edmund. 'Real terrors some of 'em. Real terrors what turns out to be scared of a mouse. Just goes to show, you can't judge by looks alone.'

'Only reason you got power is on account of

your money,' said Brogan. 'Men with money is always powerful, they can buy their power, without that you'd be no threat to anyone.'

'Probably very true,' admitted Edmund. 'But I have, and I am.'

'So powerful you got to scare women an' kids off their land?'

'Yes, I heard about you and Cora Wiesnesky. Fine lookin' woman Cora. Most men would be proud to have her,' smiled Edmund. 'Her old man walked out on her you know. He was no good for her, drunk most the time.'

'She told me,' said Brogan.

'So, you reckon you ain't a gunfighter,' said Edmund. 'Well I got two men buried on account of you not bein' a gunfighter, an' two more crippled. I don't reckon they would agree with you.'

'I said I ain't a gunfighter,' sighed Brogan. 'Though sometimes I have to stay alive. I didn't say I didn't know how to use one.'

'Point taken Brogan,' grinned Edmund. 'Yes, there is a difference, I can see that. You don't use your gun for a livin'.'

'You got it,' said Brogan. 'Your boys will testify I can use it, well, them thet's still breathin'.'

'Joe Slade must be goin' soft,' said Edmund. 'Lettin' you come in still wearin' your gun. Still, he got you here, that's the main thing.'

'He said you wanted to talk,' said Brogan.

50

'I'm listenin'.'

'Indeed I do,' replied Edmund. He slumped over his desk. 'I need men like you. Men who ain't lily-livered, who know how to handle themselves. I got me a war goin' on with some jerk named Balsam...'

'I heard,' interrupted Brogan. 'You sold him what you thought was a worn out mine, only it wasn't as worn-out as you thought.'

Edmund inclined his head again and smiled. 'That's about it, only now I want that mine back, an' I intend to have it.'

'An' Cora Wiesnesky?'

'There's gold on that land, I know it,' smiled Edmund.

'On account of some old idiot bringin' in a bag of gold. Pretty flimsy evidence I'd say. Cora says he probably found a bit here an' there over the years.'

'I gather that's what she thinks,' said Edmund. 'An' I believe her. But that gold was fresh Brogan. I can tell old stuff when I see it. Maybe she doesn't know where it is, but that old fool "Last Post" does. That's all that matters.'

'So what's the deal?' asked Brogan. 'I'm still listenin'.'

'You work for me. Help get Balsam an' Cora off their land, or sell to me. I pay you say ... Twenty dollars a week an' your keep.'

'Wouldn't get off my horse for twenty dollars

51

a week.'

Edmund smiled. 'Okay Brogan, name your price.'

'I ain't got one,' said Brogan. 'Maybe you'd find this hard to believe, but I ain't interested in money. I once turned down the chance of gettin' clear with over fifty thousand dollars. There it was for the takin'. As long as I got a few dollars in my pocket, I'm happy enough.'

Edmund seemed a little surprised. 'You refused fifty thousand? Ain't never met no man would turn down that kind of money.'

'Well you have now,' smiled Brogan. 'Right now I got fourteen dollars an' a few cents in my pocket. I don't need no more.'

'So,' smiled Edmund sitting back in his chair. 'You haven't got a cash price. So you say. You must have one, every man has his price. I learned that very early on. It's nearly always money, but, since you reckon you ain't interested in money, I gotta find out what your price is. We all got one.'

'You can try,' said Brogan. 'But I can't think of none.'

'How about fifty a week an' all found?'

'Mister Edmund,' sighed Brogan. 'You could offer fifty thousand a week. I still wouldn't be interested.'

'No,' smiled Edmund 'I don't reckon you would. You're a unique breed of man Brogan. In a way, I envy you.'

'I been driftin' since I was a boy,' said Brogan, 'I enjoy my life. Go where I please, when I please.'

'I reckon you still got a price though. I'll find it.'

'I don't aim on stayin' around for you to find out,' said Brogan.

'Oh, but you are Brogan,' smiled Edmund, suddenly producing a gun. 'I got plans for you. You see, you'll be workin' for me soon.'

'Go ahead Edmund,' goaded Brogan. 'Pull that trigger. Didn't Slade tell you I ain't afraid of dyin'? I don't want to particularly, not just yet anyhow, but if that's the way it's gotta be, I ain't bothered.'

'Yeh,' grinned Edmund. 'He told me. Don't believe him though, you neither. You'd make a good poker player Brogan. You're a good bluffer.'

'I played that too,' smiled Brogan. 'I always lost.'

Edmund gave a whistle and two men burst into the room, guns levelled at Brogan. 'Take him away, lock him in the cellar, while I think what to do.'

Brogan did not resist. His gun was taken away and he was prodded out of the room and along the corridor to a large solid door. The door was opened to reveal a long flight of steps downward. Suddenly he was crashing down the steps, landing in an aching heap. The men above simply laughed and slammed the door. Brogan found himself in complete darkness.

★   ★   ★

'At least you got to admire the guy,' said Slade sitting in the chair on the other side of Edmund's desk. 'I really do believe he's ready to die rather than do somethin' he don't want to.'

'The man's a fool then,' snapped Edmund. 'You can't tell me that any man is that ready.'

'He's a realist,' said Slade. 'He knows he's quite likely to stop a bullet one day anyhow.'

'So why did he agree to come back with you?' asked Edmund. 'He knew exactly what I wanted. If he was that fanatical he would have fought it out there an' then.'

'I didn't say he was a fanatic. Not even he's gonna deliberately get shot, he's just bidin' time.'

'There you are then,' smiled Edmund. 'He don't wanna die.'

'Reckon nobody wants to,' agreed Slade. 'What I'm sayin' is that if he has to, he will.'

'Okay then,' said Edmund. 'So we find out what'll keep him goin'. There sure must be somethin'.'

'We got no sorta lever,' said Slade. 'The threat of dyin' is enough for most men, or a threat to their family, but he ain't got none.'

'We could work him over. Maybe a good beatin' will persuade him.'

'Maybe,' said Slade doubtfully. 'Only chance you got is if he thinks he's got some sorta chance of gettin' away.'

'Then we guarantee him that chance,' said Edmund. 'He help us, an' in return we give him his freedom.'

'Think he'll buy that?'

'Why not? I know I would.'

'You ain't him.'

*　　*　　*

Brogan groped around in the dark cellar; it seemed to be filled with nothing else but racks filled with bottles, and a few barrels.

'At least I can get drunk for once in my life,' he said to himself. He stumbled across a box, which on investigation he found to contain apples and he settled himself alongside it to wait, noisily crunching the hard fruit. He supposed he must have been in there for about an hour, when the door at the top of the steps opened, sending an almost blinding light direct into his face. He covered his eyes.

'Mister Edmund wants to know if you're ready to talk again?' a silhouette at the top demanded.

'We talked already,' said Brogan.

'Seems he wants to talk some more.'

'Okay,' sighed Brogan wearily. 'If the man wants to talk. I'll listen.' He slowly climbed the steps, aware that a gun was trained on him, and walked along the cool corridor. Edmund and Slade smiled at him as he entered the room.

'Don't reckon much to the guest room,' said Brogan.

'You don't have to stay there,' said Edmund. 'I'll even give you a room in the house instead of the bunkhouse.'

'An' just what do I have to do to get such luxury?' grinned Brogan knowing the answer.

'You know very well,' replied Edmund. 'I look after my men. Slade here stays in the house too.'

'Lucky for Slade,' said Brogan. 'Does that give him a free hand with your wife as well?'

Edmund's face tightened, but he said nothing.

'No,' smiled Slade. 'Room service is extra.'

'Personally, I find a bed uncomfortable. I slept most of my life on the ground, you kinda get used to it.'

'You can sleep a few feet under, permanently, if you'd prefer,' grinned Edmund.

'No man prefer that,' said Brogan. 'But I guess if you're dead you don't notice too much. Can't do much complainin'.'

'Okay Brogan,' said Edmund. 'I know you don't trust me or anyone else round here, but

56

here's the deal. You help us get rid of Balsam an' you go free, I guarantee it.'

'Maybe you would guarantee it,' said Brogan. 'But I don't reckon Slade here will be bound by no guarantee.'

'This mornin' Brogan,' said Slade, 'I was for killin' you, even after you had helped us. Now I ain't so sure. Wouldn't be no fun no more.'

'Killin' ain't never fun,' said Brogan. 'I coulda killed Patterson an' the others outright, I had plenty opportunity, but that ain't my way. I'll kill only if I have to, an' that ain't very often.'

'Noble sentiment,' smiled Edmund. 'But a stupid one. Kill or be killed is the way it is.'

'Done me pretty well so far,' said Brogan. 'I been driftin' almost thirty years now. I've survived.'

'How many men you killed Brogan?' asked Slade.

'Some,' replied Brogan. 'I don't keep no score. If I killed them two these last two days, that's more'n I've done for maybe three years. I winged a few in that time, but that's all.'

Edmund pulled a gun out of the drawer and threw it on the desk. 'There's your gun Brogan. It's still loaded. Take it, but only if you agree to work for me. You'll be free to walk about anywhere you want, won't nobody be watchin' over you all the time.'

'An' if I just decide to ride out?'

'Ah well,' snorted Edmund placing his hands together. 'That would be most unwise. There is a limit as to how far you can go. As you saw, this place is surrounded by a high wall, guards patrol it day an' night with orders to shoot to kill if anyone tries leavin' without permission.'

'You know,' said Brogan, 'I ain't never been in prison, but I guess it can't be a whole lot worse than this place. I seen army barracks a few times, an' they got more freedom.'

'You can't carry a gun in prison,' pointed out Edmund.

Brogan grunted thoughtfully. 'I wish I could trust you Edmund, but I don't reckon I can. As soon as the dirty work was done, I reckon you'd put a bullet in my back. You or Slade.'

'Not me Brogan,' assured Edmund. 'An' Joe here, he's got a thing about bein' the fastest draw there is. Don't think he'd want to shoot you in the back, he'd want to test you.'

'Then Joe is a fool,' said Brogan. 'He knows as well as I do that that can only end up in him bein' dead, 'cos one day he'll meet somebody who is faster, or maybe he slows up for some reason, or his gun jams. It happens. I know I wouldn't put myself up against a man just to prove I was faster, nor I think would Joe. If the opposition is taken out with a bullet in the back, then there ain't no arguin' about who is the fastest, it's the one that's still alive.'

Joe Slade smiled. 'I ain't no fool.'

'Better put me back in the cellar,' said Brogan. 'I'm through listenin'.'

'Or I could kill you now,' snarled Edmund.

'Your choice,' shrugged Brogan.

'Yeh,' sneered Edmund. 'My choice. You know, here's a strange thing. I ain't never killed a man in my life. Always had someone do it for me. Maybe this once I'll give myself the pleasure. I'd like to see what it feels like.'

'Ain't nothin' to it,' invited Brogan reaching onto the desk and handing Edmund the gun. 'Just point this end at me, put your finger on the trigger an' squeeze it. BANG, an' I'm dead. At least I am if you aimed right.'

For a moment Edmund looked as if he were going to follow Brogan's instructions, and it was little relief that Brogan saw the gun waver and eventually drop onto the table.

'Hardest part is if you got the guts to actually kill a man, 'specially in cold blood an' face to face,' said Brogan. 'Believe me, the first time is always the hardest. After that, it either comes easy or you screw up altogether. Surprisin' how many just screw up.'

'You heard my terms,' snarled Edmund. 'I'll give you time to think about it. Take him back to the cellar,' he called to the two men outside the door.

This time Brogan did not give them the opportunity to knock him down the steps. Side-stepping the man about to push him, he

59

sent his fist crashing into the man's face. The man slumped into his companion, who had drawn his gun, sending the gun across the corridor.

'Hold it right there,' barked Slade from Edmund's door, gun in hand.

'I ain't tryin' to escape,' said Brogan. 'It's just these goons. I don't like bein' manhandled.'

The first man was on his feet, pulling at the gun in his holster.

'Cool it,' ordered Slade. The man sullenly replaced his gun, glancing at both Slade and Brogan. 'Okay Brogan, you go down quietly.'

'How about a lamp down there?'

'No lamp,' said Slade. 'A few hours in the dark will do you good.'

Brogan shrugged and disappeared down the steps, sitting by the box of apples again.

He must have dozed off, because suddenly he was awakened by the blinding light from the top of the steps. He could not see a thing, but the sound of footsteps did not sound like a man's boots. A slight rustle confirmed his thoughts.

Amy Edmund stood darkly above him. 'Mister McNally,' she said. 'Figured you might be hungry.' She placed a try on the box alongside him. 'Not much I'm afraid, beef stew.'

Brogan stood up and looked at the woman;

even in the dim light he could see that she was very good looking. 'Thank you Ma'am. I am feelin' a bit peckish. Apples is okay, but I don't reckon I could eat no more.'

'Don't underestimate Phil,' said Amy. 'If you don't co-operate he'll have you killed. He's used to havin' his own way.'

'Phil?' queried Brogan. 'Edmund you mean.'

'My husband,' explained Amy. 'For my sins.'

'Don't sound too happy about it.'

'Who gets what they want in this life?' she sighed. 'I guess I got most of what I want. Money, nice house, fine clothes.'

'If that's enough,' said Brogan.

'Ain't everythin',' admitted Amy. 'But I got more'n most.'

'So you get what you want an' in return you just have to be a bit of decoration for Edmund.'

'Put like that, I sound like a whore.'

'Which you probably are.'

'Was,' corrected Amy. 'He was my way out. I'd had enough of greasy fat men pawin' me. Oh, I wasn't your ordinary whore. I didn't work the saloons for two dollars a time, I came expensive.'

'Still do I reckon,' smiled Brogan.

'I get what I can out of him. I'm a realist . Who knows, one day he may throw me over for some younger woman.'

'He sent you down didn't he? Soften me up.'

'No,' smiled Amy. 'But if that's what it takes

61

to make you see sense, I don't see why not.'

'I do,' grinned Brogan. 'He'd kill me for sure, maybe you too.'

'Doubt that. He knows what the score is. I've done it for him before.'

'Slade told me you were a bit of a goer. Why should you bother what happens to me?'

'I'm just as much a prisoner here as you,' said Amy. 'Maybe more so, 'cept I know what's good for me. I do what I'm told, even if it does mean hoppin' into bed with someone now an' then. Slade talks too much anyhow.'

'I thought he had a girl in Maneheim?'

'He has. He don't get nothin' from me, that's for sure.'

'But you're ready to go with me, a dirty saddle tramp, who ain't had a bath in six months or more?'

'You interest me Mister McNally,' smiled Amy. 'Ain't often we get a man like you around. We never had one that don't seem scared of Phil or Slade. Foolish, but interesting.' She slipped her hand up to his neck. 'Think about it. Work for Phil an' you an' me, we could have a good time together.'

'I'll consider it,' replied Brogan, pushing her hand away.

A man appeared at the top of the steps. 'You okay down there Mrs Edmund?'

'Yes fine,' answered Amy. 'Just comin'.' She turned and went to the steps. 'I meant it, Mister

62

McNally.'

'I reckon you did,' agreed Brogan.

The light shone on her face and she smiled, her tongue snaking across her lips. She turned and disappeared up the steps.

'Dangerous,' muttered Brogan to himself.

'I could try persuadin' him,' suggested Amy later as she relaxed in front of the fire with her husband.

'I said I wanted none of that,' replied Edmund.

'Don't seem like your way is workin'.'

'It will,' said Edmund absently from behind a book. 'No man wants to die. He may not be scared of it, but he's just like everyone else, if there's a chance of livin', he'll take it.'

'Maybe it's as well you don't want me to try,' said Amy. 'He smells. You know I don't like men what smell.'

'How would you know?'

'I took him some food down. I noticed then that he smelled.'

'Probably never had a bath,' said Edmund. 'Men like that don't.'

'Six months he said.'

'You talked to him then?'

'Sure, if you ask me he's just about ready to be persuaded.'

'An' you'd like to persuade him, smell an' all?'

'Ain't a bad lookin' feller. Cleaned up he'd be

63

quite dishy. Let's face it. You an' I both know how it is. You know darned well I had me one of the hired hands before now.'

'Yeh, I know,' sighed Edmund. 'You're just as bad as Brogan is, maybe worse. You can play around sometimes if you like, but just let me catch you with any man who I ain't said you go with, an' I'll kill him. They know that.'

'Why do you keep me on Phil?' asked Amy. 'We both know we don't have no love for each other.'

'You want out or somethin'?'

'No, just curious. I know why I stay. But you could easy get another woman, easier than I could a rich man.'

Edmund grunted. He really did not know why he liked having her around, apart from her looks. 'Probably just to impress folk. So's I can say, "Look what I got".'

They lapsed into silence for a few minutes. 'I been thinkin',' she said, changing the subject. 'What's the only thing he's shown any interest in?'

'Nothin' as I can think of.'

'Well think a bit more.'

'Look Amy,' he said putting down his book. 'If you got somethin' on your mind, say so. But if it's lettin' you go with him, forget it.'

'No, I guess your pride wouldn't allow that,' she said. 'He already annoyed you by not givin' in. You'd hate the thought of him havin' me as

64

well.'

'So, you been thinkin',' he grunted.

'He seemed mighty taken with that Wiesnesky woman,' she said. 'But I reckon that's natural, she's more his type.'

'So?'

'So you get at him through her. Promise to let her keep her land if he co-operates with you.'

Edmund remained thoughtful for a time. 'Sometimes Amy, I think you're just as devious as me. Once in a while somethin' useful comes out of that mouth of yours.'

'How d'you think I've survived this long?' grinned Amy.

'You might just have a point,' said her husband. 'Maybe it would work. I can always get Cora's land later; even if it don't, I could get her land anyhow.'

CHAPTER FIVE

Brogan presumed that it must be morning when a tray of food was brought down, not this time by Amy, but by a surly fat cook.

'What time is it?'

'Almost seven,' responded the cook.

'Mornin' or evenin'?' asked Brogan sardonically.

'Mornin' course.'

65

'Could do with a light down here.'

'None of my business. I just do the cookin'.' The fat man dropped the tray noisily onto the apply box, spilling most of the contents of a large mug, and stomped back up the steps.

The guard, whom he assumed had been at the top of the steps all night, pulled a chair by the open door and sat astride it gazing down into the gloomy cellar. Actually, Brogan had tried the door a couple of times, but had found it firmly bolted. He had also found a hatch in the ceiling, which obviously led to the outside, but that too was firmly bolted and barred.

At least with the door open he could see to eat.

'Think the boss's got somethin' planned for you,' said his guard, seeming rather bored. 'Him an' Slade was talkin' till late about you, then Slade an' some of the boys left before dawn, don't know where they've gone, but I know it's on account of you.'

'You shouldn't have told me,' said Brogan wiping a piece of bread round his plate. 'Now you've spoiled the surprise.'

'You don't look nothin' special,' said the guard. 'But if you can take out Patterson an' Gorman, you must have somethin'. Patterson an' Gorman they was good. You killed Gorman.'

'Shoulda killed the other two as well,' replied Brogan.

'Reckon so,' agreed the guard. 'They'll be comin' after you as soon as they can, if Slade ain't killed you before then.'

Brogan decided that since he had nothing to talk about, he would just shut up and let the guard ramble on, which he did for quite some time.

Edmund appeared at the top of the steps once and, satisfied that his prisoner was still there, disappeared. Brogan did notice that he seemed unusually pleased with himself, and was somewhat surprised to be left alone.

It must have been almost noon when Edmund reappeared again. This time he seemed even more pleased.

'Okay Brogan,' he called down. 'Time to talk again.'

'What's to talk about?'

'Come on up,' laughed Edmund. 'I think you'll like talkin' this time.'

'So what's special?'

'You'll see.'

Slowly and deliberately, Brogan eased himself up the steps to face his talkative guard, now not talking, but with a gun. He was ushered along the corridor to Edmund's office, where he was offered a chair and a glass of whisky. He refused both.

Edmund smiled and nodded. 'Suit yourself. Now Brogan, I do believe we have a solution to our little impasse, a solution which should make you see sense and work for me.'

'Can't think of nothin',' said Brogan.

'Can't you?' smiled Edmund. 'I agree, your own life means very little to you, money appears to have no attraction, so what are we left with? You apparently have nobody who cares for you, or you about them.'

'You got it Edmund.'

'Indeed,' grinned Edmund. 'I believe I have. Look out of the window Brogan, tell me what you see, and then tell me if you still don't care.'

Very mystified, Brogan approached the window. It looked out onto an attractive enclosed square, containing an ornamental pool with fish and a wide variety of plants and flowers. Otherwise it was empty.

'Very nice. So what?'

Edmund joined him at the window, still smiling. 'That was a sop to my wife. Must admit, it does give the place a bit of class.' He waited silently.

A door opened on the far side.

'What the hell you playin' at?' demanded Brogan.

'Your one weakness Brogan McNally,' laughed Edmund. 'Cora Wiesnesky an' her kids.'

'What makes you think I'm bothered?'

'Intuition,' said Edmund. 'Actually it was my wife's idea; well, she had the idea that if I promised to leave Cora an' the kids alone, you'd

68

co-operate. I took it a stage further. I thought you'd be far more co-operative if I had 'em here.'

'Why should I worry? Cora already made it plain she didn't want no help.'

'She might not want you to help,' said Edmund. 'But I figured you ain't the type of man just to leave 'em to die.'

'You'd kill 'em ?'

'I'd have 'em killed,' assured Edmund. 'After I'd let my boys loose on the girls an' Cora, maybe even the boy too, no accountin' for tastes, women are scarce in this part of the world. Most my boys wouldn't be too fussy 'about the girls bein' so young, in fact they'd more likely enjoy it.'

'You'd sink that low? Didn't think any man would.'

'You'd better believe it Brogan,' said Edmund quietly, nodding to the man behind Cora. 'That way I get her land too.'

The man grinned and grabbed hold of Cora, who remained impassive.

'Tell him to leave her alone,' growled Brogan.

'They ain't had a woman in a long time,' said Edmund, opening the window and calling to the man who grudgingly let her go. 'How about it Brogan?'

'Okay,' sighed Brogan. 'Let her go back to her place. You convinced me.'

'They stay here,' said Edmund. 'Insurance. As long as I got them, I don't expect no trouble from you.'

'I want to talk to her.'

'No problem,' agreed Edmund.

'Alone.'

'Sure, why not.'

Brogan watched sadly as they were led away. 'Harm one hair on any of their heads, an' I'll kill you.'

Edmund grinned and returned to his desk, opening a drawer. 'Here.' He placed Brogan's gun on the desk. 'Go ahead, take it, it's still loaded.'

'Aint you scared I'll kill you now?'

'I'll take that chance, but if you do, Cora an' the kids will be dead before you reach the door; maybe you too.'

'Yeh, I reckon they would. Although wouldn't be much comfort to you if you was dead too.' He checked his gun and slipped it into his holster. 'My rifle too?'

'Still in your saddle in the barn.'

'Okay Edmund,' said Brogan. 'Just what is it you want me to do?'

'Get rid of Balsam.'

'On my own?'

'If you like, or you can use Slade or anyone else.'

'I'm a loner,' said Brogan. 'Don't like the idea of workin' with any of your boys. I'm

70

kinda nervous about a bullet in my back.'

'I can understand that,' admitted Edmund. 'One or two of 'em don't care too much for you.'

'Okay,' said Brogan. 'Let me see her now.'

'Follow me,' said Edmund. Outside the door, the two guards reacted very nervously at the sight of Brogan with his gun. Edmund told them it was okay, and sent them away.

At the far end of the corridor, he opened a large door and stood to one side, allowing Brogan to enter first. Cora sat by a barred window, hardly glancing at him as he came in.

'I knew it,' snarled Clem from a chair behind the door. 'You are workin' for him.'

'He is now, son,' confirmed Edmund.

'Alone,' reminded Brogan.

Edmund bowed his head, smiled and left the room.

'So he did get you,' sighed Cora. 'Told you, Edmund always gets what he wants.'

'He's been in with him all along,' sneered Clem. 'We shoulda killed him that first day.'

Brogan's initial reaction was to slap the boy down, but he resisted. He realised just how it must look to him. He walked over to the window and sat by Cora.

'How are you?'

'Oh, just fine,' said Cora. 'I always wanted to live in a big house.'

'They ain't touched you at all?'

71

'A bit of rough handlin',' said Cora. 'But I guess I'll survive that.'

'What happened?'

'As if you don't know,' sneered Clem. 'Wonder you wasn't there with 'em.'

'No,' sighed Brogan. 'I don't know, until ten minutes ago I was just as much a prisoner as you.'

Cora motioned her son to be quiet. The girls glared sullenly at Brogan, not sure if they trusted him or not. 'They came before dawn, about six of 'em. Took us all by surprise, even the dog.'

'"Last Post"?' asked Brogan.

'They didn't bother with him. Guess I should've sold out to Edmund. I knew he played dirty, I should've expected this.'

'That ain't why he took you,' said Brogan.

She looked at him disbelievingly. 'Only thing that makes sense.'

Brogan studied his feet, feeling rather ashamed. 'If I'd agreed to work for him before, there'd be no need.'

'What are you talkin' about?'

'Simple,' sighed Brogan. 'He used you to force me to work for him.'

'Why should they? We don't mean nothin' to you.'

'It was Amy Edmund's idea,' said Brogan. 'They knew they had no way of forcin' me, even threatenin' to kill me, but she guessed at my

72

one weakness. Maybe I ain't prepared to settle down with you Cora, but I got certain principles. I couldn't let anythin' happen to you or the children on account of me.'

Clem stood up angrily. 'Bullshit Mister. What you come in here for now? Talk Ma into handin' over our land?'

'Clem, I told you to be quiet!' snapped Cora. She turned watery-eyed to Brogan. 'I'd like to believe you Brogan, but I ain't sure I can now.'

Brogan shrugged. 'Can't blame you. One thing though, I ain't about to talk you into nothin'. You'll be safe as long as I do what they want.'

The girls came over to him and gave him a big hug. 'We believe you,' said Emily.

Brogan smiled weakly. 'Thanks. Right now I'm glad someone believes me. I'm gonna get you all outa here somehow. Just trust me, please.'

Cora looked at him for some time before finally choking back a sob and nodding.

'Well I don't,' snarled Clem. 'I'm gonna kill you Mister.'

'Maybe you will son,' said Brogan. 'Someone will one day I reckon, might as well be you.'

He briefly grasped Cora's shoulders before leaving the room. Edmund was waiting by the door, turning the key in the lock as Brogan came out.

'Touchin' reunion was it?' Brogan mumbled

73

something Edmund did not catch and was led back along the corridor to Edmund's office. 'Just to show I can be a man of my word.' He opened a small drawer in the desk. 'I'm gonna pay you as well.' He took out five ten-dollar bills and handed them to Brogan. 'I offered you fifty a week, so fifty it is, in advance.'

Grudgingly Brogan took the money, not because he wanted it, more to keep the peace. 'You also said somethin' about a room in the house.'

'I did indeed,' agreed Edmund. 'That's Amy's department, let's go along to the living room, she should be there.'

Some, born into wealth and position, are at one with their surroundings, there is an air of elegance and natural grace, a natural combination of furniture and people that seems quite simply, right. There are those who carry that natural grace even in the lowest of hovels. Others, even in the most luxurious of surroundings, seem at odds with those surroundings, no matter how much money they may have. Amy and Phil Edmund clashed with the trappings of their wealth.

In his travels, Brogan had seen many cases where everything seemed perfectly matched, he knew the signs well. Money can buy everything needed for the outward show, but it cannot buy that one ingredient that comes only with the years, even centuries; breeding.

74

Despite the elegance of their surroundings and fine clothes, Amy stood out garishly for what she was, a whore who had clawed her way up. Edmund himself could not control the coarseness of his upbringing. Their fine surroundings were simply a façade.

'Glad to have you with us Mister McNally.' Brogan did not bother to correct her, somehow it seemed appropriate for her to refer to him as 'Mister McNally'.

'I guess I have you to thank,' he grunted.

'Not quite what I had in mind,' smiled Amy. 'But the effect's the same.'

'Drink?' offered Edmund. Brogan declined. 'Amy, show our guest to his room. I promised him a room in the house.'

'My pleasure,' winked Amy, unseen by her husband. 'You will of course be dining with us as well. We put on a very good table.'

'I'm sure you do Ma'am.'

Amy stood up. Her husband was occupied with pouring himself a drink and had his back toward her. She preened herself, slowly and suggestively flattening out the creases in her dress, accentuating her undoubted finer points. 'Follow me Mister McNally, your room is just along the corridor.' Brogan followed, smiling to himself.

The room was comparatively small and plainly furnished, but in many ways it reflected far better taste than the ornateness of the rest of the house. A large double bed occupied most of the space, a large wardrobe much of the remainder, a chest of drawers, complete with mirror on which was a garish washbasin and a jug in a pattern of large flowers rather spoiling the appearance of the rest of the room. The view from the window was out onto the same enclosed garden he had first seen from Edmund's office.

'Not the best room in the house,' Amy almost apologised. 'But I reckon it's better than you're used to.'

'My rooms don't usually have walls an' ceilings,' was Brogan's only comment.

Amy stood by the open door provocatively, smiling softly. 'Now you're one of us, my offer still goes.'

'So you do go with the job?'

'Only your job,' she pouted. 'None of the others don't get the same.'

'I can just imagine just what your husband would do to anyone he caught as well.'

'Ain't never caught none yet.'

'An' I don't intend bein' the first. I been forced into this job, thanks to you. I'll do it, then I'll go. I ain't got interest in no comforts you got to offer.'

Amy's eyes flared. 'Prefer that tramp Cora Wiesnesky. I suppose she is more your type.'

'Cora ain't no tramp,' grated Brogan. 'She don't put on no airs an' graces either. For all

76

your money an' fine clothes, it's you that's the tramp. No hidin' that.'

Her reply to Brogan was certainly not something that would have been expected from a lady of quality and breeding, but from Amy, it seemed natural. She stormed back up the corridor, determined that Brogan McNally would bend to her will.

Brogan decided to test Edmund's assurances that he could wander about unhindered. Peering cautiously out into the corridor, he was a little surprised to find that he had no guards. Slowly and with a certain amount of defiance he ambled along the various passages and corridors, opening this door and that to see what lay behind, and to see if anyone would challenge him; none did.

There was one guard, lounging in a wicker chair outside the room Cora and the children were in. He leapt up nervously when he saw Brogan, unsure whether to go for his gun or not. Having heard of Brogan's reputation, he decided not.

'That right you're workin' for Mister Edmund now?' he asked hoarsely, keeping his hand well away from his gun.

'Sure,' grinned Brogan. 'We're all buddies together now.' The words sounded innocent enough, but the guard could not help feeling that Brogan McNally would be anything but a buddy.

Out in the huge compound that surrounded the house he attracted a few more worried glances and nudges as he walked round the various outbuildings, examining each one thoroughly.

'That's right Brogan,' said Slade behind him. 'Make yourself at home.'

Brogan had been aware of Slade following him for some time. Years of listening and waiting had conditioned Brogan to be able to almost detect the movement of a fly behind him. 'Don't nobody ever do no work round here?'

'These boys ain't workers,' explained Slade. 'Workers is in the minin' camps. We're here to see there ain't no trouble.'

'Or cause it.'

Slade shrugged. 'Maybe, but we don't dig no gold outa no mines, got a load of Chinese to do that.'

'Chinese?'

'Yeh. Boss figures Chinese is less trouble than whites or negroes. Chinese is yeller skinned an' yeller bellied right through. Must say, they work pretty damned hard too. All they need is a bowl of rice a day an' their bed, an' they're happy.'

'Where'd he get the Chinese from?'

'They came with the railroad. When that was finished, railroad company just left 'em, so Edmund took 'em on.'

'Bet they're a damn sight cheaper than whites and negroes as well.'

'Reckon so,' agreed Slade. 'That ain't our business though.'

Slade left him to wander. The last building he decided to check was the bunkhouse. He had left it until last on purpose. As he entered the gloom, a shadowy figure, arm held in a sling, blocked his way, his left hand resting on a Colt .45 he had slipped through his belt.

'As good with your left hand as with your right?' asked Brogan. 'Don't even think about it Patterson.'

'Lucky for you you is workin' for Mister Edmund now,' snarled Patterson. 'Wrong hand or not, I'd've blasted you to hell by now. Probably still will when I get the chance.'

'You tried once,' laughed Brogan. 'I reckon you got a right to try again if you want.'

'Figure you're some sort of hero, tin god or somethin',' said Patterson. 'Too good to live in the bunkhouse with the rest of the boys. You an' Slade. I heard you was sleepin' in the house. Probably got Amy to warm your bed too.'

'Could be,' agreed Brogan.

'I'll tell you this, bum,' continued Patterson. 'No matter what Edmund has promised you, I aim to see to it that you suffer for what you did to me.'

'Any time,' invited Brogan.

''Sides, it ain't in our interest to stop this war

79

with Balsam. As long as we're fightin' for him, we got a job. Same goes for Balsam's boys too. We got a kinda mutual understandin'. We shoot at each other now an' then, make it look good. Ask anybody, ain't nobody been killed yet 'ceptin' a few Chinese, but they don't matter. We can handle Slade, he don't think like us, I reckon you don't either. It might be a bit more difficult handlin' two of you.'

'Why not kill me now?'

'I ain't stupid,' growled Patterson. 'I kill you, Slade kills me. I'd watch your back when we go on a raid though, you might just become the first casualty, maybe Slade too.'

'Edmund will be very interested in all this.'

'Tell him what you like bum. I'll deny it, say you're just out to cause trouble.'

Brogan shrugged and left the bunkhouse. Frankly, he was not at all interested in why Patterson wanted to keep the war going, nor had he any real intention of fighting Balsam. He returned to the real reason for his tour of the fortress, a way to escape with Cora and her children.

Having inspected all the buildings in the compound, he turned his attention to the high wall. Two guards to each of the four sections. The main gate stood open, flanked by two more guards. The guards eyed him nervously as he stood under the white arch, gazing out onto the flat, brush covered plain that surrounded the fortress. The brush was small and did not offer much cover. Any escape attempt would have to be at night, and that meant that somehow he had to have horses on the other side, or ride through the gate.

Forming part of the wall were three buildings he had not yet inspected. The first proved to be a grain store, the second was empty, but it too showed signs of having been used for grain. The third was solidly barred and bolted, with several padlocks.

'Don't intend anyone to get in there?'

There was also another small door, again firmly locked, which obviously led outside.

'I can guess what you're thinkin',' said Slade, coming up to him. 'Mister Edmund might not like them kinda thoughts. I'd forget all about gettin' her an' the kids outa here.'

'You ain't me.'

'No,' agreed Slade. 'I'm here by choice. I'd be thinkin' the same as you in your position I reckon.'

'Can't blame a man for thinkin'.'

'Think about the Wiesnesky woman an' her kids,' reminded Slade.

'I'm thinkin',' replied Brogan.

CHAPTER SIX

'Today,' announced Slade, 'we ride out to minin' camps. Some of the boys ride out there every day, just to keep the Chinks on their toes.'

'Put the fear of God in 'em you mean,' said Brogan.

Slade smiled. 'That too probably.'

'Sounds more like a slave camp,' said Brogan. 'Thought they was hired labour?'

'Nothin' to stop 'em quittin' if they want,' smiled Slade. ''Ceptin' if they do quit we make sure they don't work nowheres else.'

Slade's meaning was obvious. Edmund did not allow his labour to just walk out.

The first camp was about ten miles away. The first four or five miles through dry scrub and then descending into wooded country along a series of small valleys. Brogan half-expected to find a prison type arrangement, and was a little surprised to find no guards and no fences. The Chinese glanced at them briefly and sullenly, but did not waver from their alloted tasks.

The mine entrance was set high up the hillside with a narrow-gauge rail track leading from it to a large shed, along which four Chinese were struggling to push a truck back up the hill, having emptied the load of gold-bearing rock in the shed, some ten more Chinese were swinging sledgehammers, breaking up the rock prior to it being shovelled into a large sluice.

They were met by a tall, fat, mean looking man, whom Slade introduced as Craig Thomas, the foreman.

'So you're the new boy,' grunted Thomas. 'Just let me get things straight. I'm in charge here. No matter what you see or hear, it ain't none of your business.' He sounded almost resentful of their presence. 'I have certain rules. No talkin' to the chinks, no askin' questions, an' most of all keep your sticky fingers off any gold you see. Any man, an' that includes you, caught with gold in his pockets, gets shot.'

'Got it,' assured Brogan. 'Just what the hell we doin' here?'

'I ask myself the same question frequently,' said Thomas. 'But Mister Edmund wants it that way. As far as I'm concerned your job is just to catch the odd runaway.'

'Get many?' asked Brogan.

'Some,' admitted Thomas. 'Mainly the young uns. We had to shoot one day before yesterday. Tried to get away with a bag full of gold.'

'He was caught about five miles out,' explained Slade. 'Boys brought him back here. We always make 'em all watch the shootin', just to show 'em they can't get away with it.'

'Supposin' one leaves without any gold?'

'Floggin' usually,' said Slade. 'The first time anyhow. Second time we usually shoot 'em.'

'He run away?' Brogan pointed to an elderly, thin, Chinese bent over the sluice, his back covered in fresh looking scars.

'Him?' laughed Thomas. 'Naw. Tried to pretend he was sick. Refused to work. We convinced him he wasn't sick at all.'

'They must get sick sometimes.'

'Sometimes,' admitted Thomas. 'But they know better.'

'Ain't there no law around here?'

'This is the only law,' said Slade slapping his gun. 'An' Mister Edmund.'

Thomas was called away, leaving Slade and Brogan to wander round the camp. Down a muddy slope were various huts, obviously the homes of the workers, and Brogan caught a glimpse of a woman ushering a child into the safety of her hut as they approached.

'You got women here too?' asked Brogan.

'About twenty, an' about ten kids,' replied Slade.

'Thought Edmund said there wasn't no women hereabouts.'

'Don't count 'em as women,' said Slade. ''Sides, Thomas don't allow us nowhere near 'em. Edmund don't like it either.'

'How come? Wouldn't have thought he'd been bothered.'

'Funny people these Chinks,' said Slade.

84

'They'll take all sorts of beatin's, even accept the floggin's an' shootin's. Touch one of their women though an' they'll turn into a mob of howlin' maniacs. Couple of fellers tried it not long ago, we found their bodies in the river, hacked to death with shovels.'

'Edmund accept that?'

'Had to. Gold's more important than a couple of lives. Messin' about with their women is one sure way of stoppin' 'em workin', an' Edmund don't like 'em not workin', so we leave 'em alone.'

'I hear you got a girl in Maneheim.'

'Better'n nothin',' shrugged Slade.

'You don't mind her bein' a whore? She tried to get me to go with her.'

'Tried?' asked Slade.

'Yeh, I told her to beat it.'

'Must be the first refusal she ever had,' grinned Slade. 'Naw, I ain't bothered. Got to make a livin' best she can.'

'Fat Pete, the bartender, he said you wouldn't like it.'

'If you went with her?'

'No. 'Cos I told her where to go.'

Slade shrugged. 'If you didn't want to, what's to mind? I don't reckon on takin' her with me when I go.'

'You goin' then?'

'Expect so,' replied Slade. 'Don't know when though.'

They had climbed up to the mine entrance and had to jump out of the way as a tirade of Chinese abuse and the rumble of a truck full of rock came hurtling out of the mine and down the slope.

'Got no respect,' said Slade. 'That's the trouble with 'em. Wouldn't bother them if you was killed by that truck. Probably even did it on purpose.'

'Got their jobs to do,' observed Brogan. 'You say there's another camp?'

'Down the valley,' said Slade. 'Much the same as this. Thomas is in charge there too.'

'Where's Balsam's place?'

'Seely Flats. About ten miles south.'

'I'd like to see it,' said Brogan. 'If I'm to get rid of Balsam I need to know the layout.'

'No problem,' said Slade. 'We'll ride out there after we've had somethin' to eat.'

'He use Chinese too?'

'Yeh, but he lives on the camp.'

'Accordin' to Patterson, the rest of the boys ain't got no interest in gettin' rid of Balsam. Says as long as the war is goin' on they got jobs.'

'I know that. So does Edmund, so does Balsam I reckon. That's why he wanted you. You an' me, we ain't got that interest.'

'Thought you would.'

'Sure it's a good job, pays well,' admitted Slade. 'But the others know darned well that when it's finished, so are they. Me, I reckon I'd be kept on. You, you only want to get away.'

'I could leave right now.'

'Go ahead,' said Slade. 'Edmund would carry out his threat to Cora an' her kids. He don't make idle promises.'

'Nor do I,' said Brogan. 'An I ain't leavin' without 'em.'

After a passable meal, Brogan and Slade set off down the valley through the second camp, almost an exact replica of the first, and on toward Seely Flats. Eventually, Slade led the way off the main track and up the side of the valley, leaving the wooded slopes behind, following a narrow track until he pulled up.

'Down there,' Slade pointed over the edge of a high cliff.

Some two hundred feet below, spreadeagled across the river, was another camp, smaller than either of the other two. On the other side of the river, a little way up a slope among the trees was a large house.

'Balsam's?' asked Brogan.

'Balsam's,' confirmed Slade. 'Them huts on this side is for his workers. Entrance to the mine is in them trees up to the right.'

Brogan could just make out a set of rail tracks snaking toward a large shed. 'He got guards posted?'

'Sure,' said Slade. 'Day an' night. He needs 'em, we don't. Don't reckon he's got any plans

87

on any of Edmund's mines, but he knows for sure Edmund is after him.'

'Don't look easy for a direct attack,' said Brogan. 'Plenty of cover. They could hold out forever.'

'We got more men than him. We could take 'em.'

'Not if the others ain't interested.'

'That's the problem,' sighed Slade. 'Looks like it's up to us two, maybe a couple of others.'

'Thought of causin' a landslide? Few sticks of dynamite would soon set this lot movin'.' He tapped the rock.

'Tried it a couple of times,' said Slade. 'Too many trees. Damage it done was nothin'.'

'Probably right,' said Brogan, not really interested. He had ridden out for appearances' sake.

They twisted their way back to camp to be met with a certain amount of excitement. The Chinese were all being herded into an open space behind the big shed.

'What's goin' on?' asked Brogan.

Thomas answered his question as he walked over to them, smiling broadly. 'Found some gold hidden in one of the huts. We do spot checks now an' then.'

Before Brogan could ask any more questions, two of Thomas's men pushed a struggling youth out of one of the huts, his hands firmly tied behind him. He fell to the ground several times, only to receive savage kicks from his two captors. Eventually he was tied to a post alongside the river.

'You're in luck,' smiled Slade. 'We're gonna have us a shootin'.'

Brogan grunted as the rest of the Chinese labourers, their women and their children were herded in. 'You mean he's outa luck.'

'He knows the rules,' said Thomas. 'They all do, but that don't seem to stop 'em doin' it. They think they can beat the system.'

'Any ever get away with it?'

'Odd one now an' again.'

The youth had stopped struggling and was now glaring defiantly at the three of them. An elderly woman suddenly rushed out of the crowd, screaming and shouting, and threw her arms around the youth. There was no attempt to stop her, simply sneers of contempt. Eventually the woman was pulled away and pushed roughly back into the crowd.

'His mother I take it,' said Brogan.

'Must be, I reckon,' answered Slade. 'Job to know. We don't keep no check on things like that.'

The woman rushed out again, tears streaming down her face and grovelled at Thomas's feet, pleading with him in Chinese. Thomas kicked her away, answering her in faltering Chinese.

'You speak their language,' observed Brogan.

'Picked it up,' grinned Thomas. 'Had to.

They pretend they don't understand English when it suits 'em.'

'So what happens now?' asked Brogan as the two men hauled the screaming woman away.

'He gets shot,' replied Thomas simply.

'An' you got the job of shootin' him,' laughed Slade.

Brogan turned angrily. 'I don't do nothin'. I ain't got no quarrel with him or any of them.'

'Mister Edmund ain't gonna like that,' grinned Slade.

'I don't give a damn what Edmund likes or dislikes. I agreed to work for him to get Balsam. I ain't never killed nobody in cold blood yet, an' I ain't about to start now. Let the boy go.'

Thomas laughed. 'Since when did you give the orders? Mister, you do like you're told.'

Brogan's gun was in his hand, pointed at Thomas's belly. 'I said let the boy go.'

'You aim to kill me?' asked Thomas somewhat nervously.

'If I have to. Let the boy go an' that won't be necessary.' He turned to the rest of the men. 'An' don't get no fancy ideas. Probably you can kill me, but Thomas here gets it first. Cut the boy loose.'

Thomas looked appealingly at Slade. 'Reckon he means it?'

'He means it,' shrugged Slade. 'The man's loco.'

Thomas turned to his two men and nodded;
90

reluctantly, they cut the youth free.

'Boy,' called Brogan. 'You understand English?' The youth nodded. 'Get on that horse over there an' get the hell outa here.'

The youth stared disbelievingly at Brogan, convinced that it must be some sort of trick. A shout from the woman brought him out of his trance and he leapt on the horse and galloped off as fast as he could. Thomas's men raced for two other horses to give chase, but a warning shot from Brogan brought them to a standstill.

'We wait here,' he ordered. 'We all wait here, give the boy time to get clear. Anyone got other ideas, forget 'em. I don't miss very often.'

'How long you intend keepin' us here?' asked Slade.

'About an hour should do,' said Brogan. 'Okay, the rest of you, drop your guns. We might as well wait in comfort; into the office.'

They all filed into the office and Brogan took up position by the door. The Chinese burst into a frenzy of babbling conversation but stayed where they were, unsure what to make of this strange man.

'If the boy's got any sense,' said Brogan. 'He'll head for Balsam's camp.'

'Yeh,' grinned Slade. 'Probably will. Balsam's soft with 'em. Some of 'em already ended up there.'

'You just made one big mistake Mister,' snarled Thomas.

'Maybe,' agreed Brogan. 'But I'll take that chance.'

'If I was you Mister,' continued Thomas, 'I'd ride out after the boy an' join Balsam yourself. You're a dead man. I'll see to that.'

'You can try,' invited Brogan.

During all this time, Slade had made no attempt to stop Brogan. Actually he was quite amused by the whole episode. One or two of his men looked to Slade for guidance at first, but he had motioned them to do nothing. Only Thomas's two men had seemed intent on trying anything, but they had heard of Brogan's reputation.

'Do somethin' Slade,' demanded Thomas 'That's your job.'

'Like what?' asked Slade. 'We none of us got no guns.'

'Very wise,' said Brogan.

'Edmund will deal with him,' assured Slade. 'He ain't gonna like this one bit.'

Brogan kept them waiting for a good hour before finally relaxing. 'I reckon he's well away by now. Okay, let's get back an' see what Edmund has to say.'

'Don't ever show your face here again,' growled Thomas. 'I'll kill you if you do.'

The woman rushed and threw herself at Brogan's feet, sobbing her thanks hysterically. Brogan pulled her to her feet and smiled at her. 'That's okay,' he soothed. He turned to the rest

92

of the Chinese. 'Don't count on me bein' around again next time though.'

Thomas and his two men watched sullenly as Brogan led the way, tempted to go for their guns, but they resisted.

'Oh, an' don't let me hear of you takin' it out on the rest of them,' called Brogan. 'They ain't done nothin'.'

'I'll say this for you Brogan,' said Slade pulling alongside. 'You got some guts. We coulda killed you.'

'Then why didn't you?'

'Let's just say I'm kinda curious to know just what makes you tick, how far you're prepared to go.'

'Won't Edmund be mad at you for not stoppin' me?'

'Probably, but I can live with that. Question is, will you be able to live with it?'

'As long as Edmund thinks I'm any use to him.'

'I guess so,' grinned Slade. 'I don't reckon one Chink is gonna alter that.'

The silence when Brogan walked into Edmund's office was overpowering. Slade had explained what had happened and, as expected, Edmund was far from pleased. For some considerable time he sat back in his leather chair and stared hard at Brogan. The two men behind the door had relieved Brogan of his gun as soon as he walked in. He had expected that.

93

Edmund angrily tapped his fingertips together. 'I ought to have you shot instead,' he rasped eventually. 'Just what the hell do you mean by interferin' in my business?'

'You may be able to force me to work for you Edmund . . .'

'Mister Edmund to you McNally,' interrupted Edmund.

Brogan shrugged. 'Okay MISTER Edmund . . . Like I said, you may be able to force me to work for you against Balsam, but that's all. Nobody can force me to kill an innocent man . . .'

'Innocent?' roared Edmund. 'Innocent. That thievin' Chink had more'n four ounces of my gold hidden away. I don't call that innocent.'

Brogan grinned and flopped into a chair. 'How much you payin' 'em for slavin' their guts out?'

'That's my business,' glowered Edmund. 'They get looked after.'

'By a whip or a bullet,' said Brogan. 'Don't reckon much on them kinda wages.'

'You had no right to interfere,' barked Edmund. 'Any other man an' you'd be buzzard meat by now.'

'But I ain't yet,' grinned Brogan again. 'I reckon you still got use for me, otherwise I would be buzzard meat.'

'Don't push your luck McNally. From now on you do just what you're told, even if it does

94

mean shootin' a bloody Chink.'

'No chance MISTER Edmund; 'sides, Thomas said he'd kill me if I show my face again.'

'So you could've refused to kill him,' snarled Edmund. 'One of the others would've. How I run my business is no concern of yours.'

'Better tell Thomas to be careful,' warned Brogan. 'Or you might end up with more'n just a few dead Chinese. Nothin' would suit Balsam better'n havin' a squabble in your own camp.'

'I'll deal with Thomas,' snapped Edmund. 'But first I gotta show that you ain't gettin' away with it. I reckon a taste of the whip will do you good. Take him outside, I want to watch this.'

Before he could move, Brogan was seized by the two guards and dragged from the room and out into the compound.

'Get the Wiesnesky woman,' Edmund ordered Slade. 'This'll do her good as well.'

'Might have more effect on Brogan if you gave her a good whippin' instead,' observed Slade. 'I don't reckon whippin' him will make a whole lot of difference.'

'Maybe not,' agreed Edmund. 'But it sure will give me some satisfaction. No, we don't hurt her, not yet anyhow. I reckon it would just make him worse.'

'I told you from the start he wasn't to be trusted,' said Slade. 'He just ain't worth it.'

'I'll be the judge of that,' snapped Edmund.

'If I can't buy a man, then I'll get him some other way. Now get that woman.'

Slade did not argue any more, he knew better. How Edmund chose to run his business was none of his affair.

Brogan had been spreadeagled across a large wagon wheel leaning against a wall, his shirt ripped from his back, arms and legs securely tied. Jim Patterson stood close by, arm still in the sling, leering at him.

'Crossed Edmund again have you?' he laughed. 'Don't do to cross Mister Edmund. I hope he has you whipped to death.'

'Bet you wish you was doin' it yourself,' said Brogan.

'I still can. I can whip you okay with my left hand.'

'Then maybe you'd better,' said Brogan. ''Cos it's the only chance you're ever gonna get.'

There was a disturbance among the men gathered round. Brogan twisted his neck and saw Cora being pushed to the front. 'No need for her to see this,' he said.

'An' I think there is,' replied Edmund from somewhere behind him. 'Next time it'll be her on that wheel while you watch, if you step out of line once more.'

'Leave him alone,' cried Cora. 'You can have my land, I'll give it to you.'

'I'll get that too,' laughed Edmund. 'Sorry

Cora, but right now I need him more'n I need your land.'

'Mighty peculiar way you have of showin' it,' grinned Brogan.

'You won't die,' assured Edmund. 'This is just to whip you into line so to speak.'

'Boss,' said Patterson. 'Let me do it. I'll give him the biggest whippin' he ever had.'

'See,' smiled Edmund. 'I even got me a volunteer.'

'Better let him do it,' said Brogan. 'Only chance he's ever gonna get, he's already a dead man.'

'That's between you an' him,' laughed Edmund. 'Okay, let Jim have the whip. Mind now, I don't want him dead.'

'Pity,' snarled Patterson. 'Still, I'm gonna enjoy this.' The rawhide whip was passed to Patterson, who proceeded to crack it ominously.

'Get on with it,' grated Brogan. 'We can all see you know how to use it.'

'I want you to think about it first,' gloated Patterson. 'Think about it bitin' into your back. Think about the pain McNally. I was whipped once an' I can assure you it wasn't very nice. I want you to beg for mercy, an' you can beg all you like, 'cos I ain't gonna be merciful.'

'I'll die first,' hissed Brogan. 'Maybe you'd better kill me, 'cos I aim to finish you off.'

Suddenly the whip streaked across his bare

97

back, making him arch in agony, but he was determined not to give Patterson the satisfaction of crying out. The whip flashed a second time, this time Brogan hardly able to contain the cry within his throat. His teeth bit into the wooden spoke of the wheel by his face. The whip crashed a third time.

'Beg!' yelled Patterson. 'Come on McNally, beg for mercy!' Brogan bit deeper into the wood.

The whip hissed through the air again. Cora collapsed.

CHAPTER SEVEN

He knew he had opened his eyes, but all about him was black. He moved slightly, only to bring a sharp wince of pain as his back seemed to crack open. He tried rolling over, but when he did eventually manage it the searing torn flesh could not stand his weight, so he eased back onto his stomach, sighing with relief.

A faint musty smell told him where he was, in the cellar, the odour coming from the box of apples. How long he had been there, or what time it was, he had no idea.

After some considerable time, he was able to steel himself and climb agonisingly to his feet. His back touched one of the racks and made him double up in agony. After that he made sure that nothing touched his back. He found the box of apples and sat on it, flexing his back slightly to try to relieve the stiffness.

Something sharp between his teeth reminded him of biting into the spoke of the wheel, and he slowly removed the offending piece of wood. As far as he could remember he had not given Patterson the satisfaction of crying out, although he did not even remember blacking out.

His mouth and throat felt very dry. He needed a drink, and since there only appeared to be bottles of wine in the cellar, at least as far as he could remember, he groped for the nearest shelf and caught hold of a bottle. Not having the means to pull the tightly-wedged cork out, he smashed the neck of the bottle and gingerly tasted the liquid.

'Not bad,' he mused to himself. 'Better'n nothin'.' He took a longer drink.

He had the idea of smashing every bottle he could find, but eventually decided it would serve no useful purpose. Having satisfied his thirst, he made his way to where he knew the trapdoor was above him. In one corner he could just make out a very faint glimmer of light and fumbled around the floor for something to stand on, eventually finding a barrel which he painfully manoeuvred into position. By chance he also found a bale hook hanging on the wall close by.

Standing a little unsteadily on the barrel, he was able to use the bale hook to chip away at the tiny hole, until at last it was big enough for him to see through. There was little to be seen, except the odd pair of legs walking by. The occasional voice came and went.

The sound of the lock turning in the door at the top of the steps made him resume his position on the apple box. In the glare of the lamplight descending the stairs, he made out two figures and from the rustle of material, assumed one of them to be Amy Edmund.

'So you're alive,' came Edmund's voice from behind the glare of the lamp. 'Had us kinda worried for a while.'

'Why should you worry?' asked Brogan.

'I didn't want you dead,' replied Edmund. 'Patterson got carried away, we had to pull him off.'

'Thanks for nothin',' said Brogan. 'You shoulda let him finish it.'

'Don't be silly Mister McNally,' said Amy Edmund. 'You'd be no use to anyone dead.'

'Don't reckon on bein' much use to anyone alive.'

'Remember we still got Cora Wiesnesky,' reminded Edmund.

Brogan grunted. He remembered and was beginning to wonder if it was worth it.

'Let me look at your back,' said Amy. 'I got

100

some ointment to put on it.'

'Reckon I'll survive without that.'

'Do as you're told,' ordered Edmund. 'I got plans for you.'

His back was still very sore, so he turned grudgingly for them to see, wincing slightly as Amy's hand touched it.

'I seen worse,' she said. 'Hold still now while I put this ointment on. It'll sting a bit at first, but it'll clean the wounds.' Brogan braced himself. She was right, it did sting and he felt under no compulsion not to let it be known it stung. Gradually, the stinging changed to a warm soothing feeling which seemed to relax the taut muscles.

'I helped myself to one of your bottles of wine,' said Brogan. 'Seems there's nothin' much else to drink down here.'

'I can see that,' said Edmund picking up the bottle with the broken neck. 'Chose one of the best I see.'

'Only the best is good enough,' said Brogan.

'I'll get some food an' coffee sent down,' said Amy, eventually satisfied that she had applied sufficient ointment.

'You keepin' me down here?'

'For the moment,' said Edmund.

'How about a lamp?'

'Brogan, I may not be the brightest person in the world, but even I know that a lamp with all this alcohol would be dangerous.'

101

'Wine don't burn.'

'There's other stuff besides wine,' said Edmund. 'No, you stay in the dark for a while.'

'What time is it?'

'About eight in the mornin',' replied Amy.

'I been out since yesterday?'

'You were a bit delirious early on,' said Edmund, 'but you calmed down. Patterson did a good job. Maybe too good.'

'I'd keep that man outa my way if I was you,' snarled Brogan. 'I meant what I said about him bein' a dead man.'

'Deal with Balsam first, then you can do what you like with Patterson.'

Brogan was tempted to tell Edmund that he too was at the top of his list, but decided not to. It would do him no good at the moment. Edmund and Amy left but the guard took up position at the top of the steps, letting some light into the cellar. This was a different guard, not talkative as the other had been.

About twenty minutes later the fat cook appeared with a tray of food and some coffee, again succeeding in spilling most of it. After he had eaten, Brogan took the opportunity to look about the cellar, finding out exactly what was in there. The guard watched him disinterestedly, making no attempt to stop him.

'At least I got the choicest wines to drink,' called Brogan, smashing the neck of another bottle. 'Want some?'

The guard glared down at him in silence. Brogan took a drink of what proved to be red wine, the same as before. He had never tasted a good wine, only home-made or cheap stuff in a couple of saloons when there had been no beer, and even his unsophisticated palate could appreciate the difference.

'Ain't you supposed to stop me or somethin'?' he called to his guard.

'None of my concern,' muttered the guard.

'That's what I like. A dedicated man,' grinned Brogan.

An examination of the barrels, including the one he had been standing on, proved very interesting. WOOD ALCOHOL proclaimed the letters on the side.

'So this is what Edmund was worried about,' he said to himself.

Further search produced a crowbar and a bundle of rags. There was little else of interest, the rest of the shelving being taken up with wine.

'How long they keepin' me down here?' he called again.

'Another day from what I hear,' replied the guard.

Brogan slid the crowbar alongside the barrel he had been standing on, wandered round the cellar some more and finally sat down on the apple box, absently munching one of them.

Half an hour later the cook returned to take

away the tray and the guard shut the door. An idea grew in Brogan's mind. He found the rags again and arranged them against a wall, moved the apple box and made himself comfortable.

He had two other visits from Edmund, one in company with Amy who examined his wounds and applied some more ointment and another visit from the cook at about seven in the evening with his meal, which was once again eaten by the light of the door. He settled down to get some sleep.

When he woke again he made his way to the trapdoor and looked out. It was dark but clear. He could make out a few stars in the sky. Using the crowbar, he managed to make the hole big enough to get an arm through. It seemed that the doors were held by a long wooden bar, quite thick and heavy and he was unable to move it. He chipped again at the hole.

The noise at the top of the steps as the key turned in the lock had him rushing back to his makeshift bed. A shadowy figure behind a lamp came down the steps.

'Just checkin',' said Slade. 'I see you made yourself comfortable.'

'I slept in worse,' said Brogan. 'What time is it?'

'Almost eleven. We're all turnin' in now. You'll be out of here in the mornin'. We got work to do.'

'What's that?'

'We're gonna try an all-out attack on Balsam.' Slade laughed. 'But don't you get no ideas. I'll be right behind you, an' even though I quite like you, I'll kill you.'

'I don't doubt it,' said Brogan. 'Can the condemned man have a request?'

'Depends,' said Slade.

'I could do with a smoke, just one.'

Slade grunted. 'Ain't supposed to let you have nothin'.'

'Aw, c'mon,' pleaded Brogan. 'What harm can one lousy smoke do?'

Slade thought about it for a time. 'Okay, just one, but don't you go tellin' Edmund mind.'

'I won't,' assured Brogan.

Slade took a long thin cheroot out of his pocket and handed it to Brogan, lifting the lamp glass for him to light it. Brogan pretended to draw gratefully. He was strictly a non-smoker and the taste and smoke made him choke. 'Strong stuff,' he wheezed.

'I like 'em strong,' said Slade. 'I hear you been drinkin' Edmund's best wine?'

'Might as well,' said Brogan. 'Ain't nothin' clse to do down here.'

Slade laughed and disappeared up the steps. The door slammed and the key turned in the lock. The first thing Brogan did was to try to light some of the rags. It proved more difficult than he had expected, but after ten minutes the rags started to blaze. He ripped apart the apple

105

box and soon had a fire going, the light of which helped him to get around.

For another half-hour he patiently chipped away at the hole, until it was big enough for him to get his head through. The moon was high and bright and with great dismay he realised that the bar across the shutters was firmly padlocked. There was only one course open. He had to enlarge the hole sufficient to be able to squeeze through.

Just as he was about to start again, a noise on the rough dry earth made him freeze. Peering cautiously through the hole, he was horrified to see an armed guard standing nearby, apparently looking straight at the hole.

'The fire,' thought Brogan. 'It's a dead giveaway.' He turned his body to try to shield the glow from the hole and waited tensely. Suddenly the guard turned on his heels and crunched slowly away. There was no time to lose, he had to get out quickly.

Risking attracting attention, he forced the crowbar into the splintered wood and broke more timber. A little surprised, he found that he soon had made a hole big enough to squeeze through, without anyone hearing.

Going back into the cellar, he smashed the bar through the tops of the four barrels of wood alcohol and spilled the contents over the floor. He had noticed that the cellar ceiling was wood, and from what he remembered it must have been directly underneath Edmund's living room. He splashed a liberal amount of the alcohol up onto the wooden ceiling and over the shelves. There was a slight slope of the floor which made it impossible for the liquid to reach the fire. He placed some more wood on the fire, fully intending to come back later and kick it into the alcohol.

Taking the crowbar with him he forced himself through the opening, tearing his back as he did, causing him to freeze in agony. Alongside the cellar trapdoor he found an old piece of oilcloth, which he spread out over the hole. A quick look round indicated that it was all clear, the only signs of life being a guard on the gate and two on the walls, quite some distance away.

The stables were round the side of the house, between it and the wall, and he raced round under cover of the shadows, only having to cross a short patch of open ground alongside the stable, which he managed without being seen. His horse and saddle, still complete with rifle, were there, along with several other saddles and a couple of rifles. Quietly but quickly, he saddled four horses and made sure the stable door was unfastened.

He slipped along in the shadows towards the gate. The guard was lounging on the other side and there seemed to be no way Brogan could get to him without being seen. He decided to brazen it out.

Stepping out of the shadows he walked openly and slowly toward the guard. 'That you Slim?' whispered the guard. Brogan grunted and walked forward. 'What the hell you doin' without your shirt?' By now Brogan was almost on top of his man. 'Hey, you ain't Slim, you're . . .' His interest in who it was ended as Brogan crashed the butt of his rifle into the man's face, following it up with a blow from the crowbar. Brogan felt rather than heard the bone splinter.

A quick search of the body did not produce the keys to the two padlocks and he set to prising the locks off their mountings. They came away remarkably easily and he eased the gate open slightly and dragged the body outside, leaving it in a pool of dark shadow. Then he returned to the compound, closing the gate arranging the padlocks to make it look as if they were still intact.

'That's the easy part over with,' he grunted to himself. 'Now to get Cora.'

He could have simply walked through the front door of the house, but he knew that there was probably a guard, if not actually at the cellar door, very close by, and almost certainly one on Cora's room. From the front door, there was a long passage which he had to get down to surprise his guard. It would be easier from the other direction.

The only other way to get to her was to go up

onto the roof, into the enclosed garden, and through the door by her room. Luckily, the house was only a single-story affair with a flat roof.

A narrow flight of steps led up to the roof from by the stables, the only problem being that he would be in full view of the guard patrolling the wall, not thirty feet away. Brogan crouched at the top and waited. It seemed that the guard was more than happy to stay where he was. However, after about ten minutes, he turned and ambled slowly along the wall, his back now turned to the house. Brogan was quick to take the opportunity to cross the flat roof and lower himself into the garden.

Apart from two dim lights, one where he assumed the cellar guard was positioned and the other outside Cora's door, the house was in darkness. The door leading to the corridor by Cora's room was mercifully unlocked and he quietly eased himself through.

As he had expected, there was a guard outside the room, slumped down in the wicker chair, snoring gently, rifle across his knees. A swing of the crowbar ensured that the guard did not wake up.

Brogan eased himself into the room. 'Cora,' he called softly. 'Cora, it's me, Brogan.'

At first there was no answer. 'Mister Brogan?' Emily, the youngest, sat up in bed sleepily rubbing her eyes. 'Have you come to take us home Mister Brogan?'

'Sure thing Emily,' he whispered. 'Where's your Ma?'

'In here, with me,' whispered Emily excitedly, now wide awake. She shook her mother. 'Mam, Mam, it's Mister Brogan. He's come to take us home.'

'Home,' mumbled Cora. Suddenly she sat up. 'Brogan? It is you isn't it?' Brogan assured her it was. 'Are you okay? I was worried about you. I thought they'd killed you.'

'I'm okay,' he assured again. 'Bit sore, but okay. Come on, I've got horses waitin'.'

Cora woke up the others but Clem, suddenly realising it was Brogan, started to call out. Instinctively Brogan's fist slammed into the boy's face, effectively silencing him.

'Sorry about that boy,' apologised Brogan. 'But I can't have you givin' the game away.'

Cora anxiously examined her son. 'No need to do that,' she whispered.

'There was an' you know it,' said Brogan. 'I had to, he'd have given us away for sure.' Cora did not argue. 'Come on now, we've got to get past at least one more guard. I'll carry him, you get the rifle an' gunbelt off the guard outside.'

Cora and the girls crept out of the room, the two girls stifling a cry of horror when they saw the bloodstained guard slumped on the floor. Cora quickly unfastened the gunbelt and handed it back to Brogan who fastened it round

110

his waist, taking the rifle herself. Brogan picked up the boy and tossed him over his shoulder, wincing slightly as the weight reminded him of his wounds.

'Quickly now, follow me,' he whispered.

They obediently followed Brogan along the cool corridor until he motioned them to remain where they were. Slowly lowering Clem, he eased himself to the corner and peered round. His guard appeared to be asleep in his chair. He took a tight grip of the crowbar and crept forward. The crowbar swung, making a sickening crunch as the skull splintered. He lowered the guard to the floor and picked up the oil-lamp.

Slowly opening the cellar door, he went down a few steps and hurled the lamp as hard as he could at where he knew the wood alcohol was, and watched for a moment in satisfaction as the flames spread rapidly. Then he locked the door again, picked up the still unconscious Clem and motioned Cora and the girls to follow.

Outside, all seemed quiet with no sign of any guards. Quickly, under cover of the shadows, they made their way to the stables where he pushed Clem across his horse and helped Cora and the girls on to the others.

'Now we wait a bit,' he whispered. 'I started a fire in the cellar. It should cause quite a diversion.' Peering through a crack, he watched patiently. It seemed an eternity before anything started to happen.

'Phil,' cried Amy shaking her husband. 'Phil, I smell smoke.'

'What you talkin' about?' mumbled Edmund.

'Smoke,' repeated Amy. 'Somethin's burnin'.'

Edmund smelled it too and was now wide awake, leaping from bed and out into the corridor. Smoke was seeping under the door of the living room and he burst in. He was almost instantly forced back as the draught from the open door fanned the flames leaping up from the floor.

'Christ,' he spluttered realising just where the fire had started. 'Brogan McNally. What the hell is he up to?'

By now Slade too was in the corridor, groping through the now dense smoke. 'He started this,' he choked. 'I told you he was no good, I'll get the bastard.'

'Get everybody out the house first,' ordered Edmund. 'McNally will die for this.'

Slade raced along the corridor, tripping over the body of the guard by the cellar door. Picking himself up, he tried the door, somewhat surprised to find it locked. At the top of the steps he shielded his eyes from the glare and heat and called out, not really expecting an answer.

'The Wiesnesky woman,' he choked and ran

112

along the corridor to her room. The smoke had not yet reached this end of the house and what he found came as no surprise. The guard dead and the room empty.

'He's got Cora an' the kids,' he called out as he met Edmund.

The flames had burst through the cellar trapdoor, muffled explosions came from below as bottles of wine burst under the heat. Suddenly the whole area was alive as people ran toward the house, which was now well alight. Thoughts of Brogan disappeared from Edmund's mind as he raced about screaming to everyone to get water to put the fire out.

'He can't have got far,' panted Slade. 'I'll take some of the boys an' go after him.'

'To hell with McNally!' ranted Edmund. 'We'll get him later, set everyone puttin' the fire out.'

Slade shrugged. In a way he admired Brogan, half-hoping he would get away. He organised the men into a chain, passing buckets of water from the well; even the guards off the wall joined in.

This was Brogan's signal that it was time to make a run for it and he opened the stable door and ordered the others to follow him. In the confusion, nobody seemed to notice four horses heading for the gate. Brogan pulled the locks away, opened the gates and they all rode swiftly through.

The human chain and their buckets were fighting an impossible battle. It soon became obvious to all except Edmund that their futile efforts were having no serious effect whatsoever. Edmund however insisted that they carry on.

'Forget it Boss,' urged Slade. 'It's hopeless.'

'McNally,' panted Edmund. 'I'm gonna kill him with my own bare hands. He's gonna die real slow for this.'

'We got to get after 'em,' urged Slade again.

Eventually Edmund came to realise that there was no chance of saving the house. Amy stood gazing at the unstoppable flames, complaining and sobbing about her lost jewellery. Edmund stood stunned for some time.

Slade started to round up the men and ordered them to get their horses.

'Forget it,' barked Edmund. 'We got no chance of findin' 'em in the dark. Wait till dawn.'

Edmund made sense, so Slade ordered the men to move the horses well away from the encroaching flames. He walked over to the gate, grinned slightly when he saw how easily the lock mountings had been broken and found the body of the guard outside.

'Good luck Brogan,' he smiled to himself. 'You're gonna need it.'

CHAPTER EIGHT

'You get back to your place,' panted Brogan after they had been riding for about half an hour. 'Dig yourselves in.'

'Where you goin'?' asked Cora.

'The mine,' replied Brogan. 'Cause a bit of a diversion.'

Clem had now recovered, glaring hatred at Brogan, his jaw swollen and stiff from Brogan's swift attentions. 'First place they'll look is our place,' he growled.

'Maybe,' said Brogan. 'But I don't reckon they'll start out before dawn, by that time they should've had a message from the mining camp. Right now it's me that Edmund wants a hell of a lot more'n you. How's the jaw?'

'Not busted,' snarled Clem. 'No thanks to you.'

'Sorry boy,' said Brogan. 'I had to do it, you'd've raised the alarm for sure.'

'Too right I would,' glared Clem. 'They'd probably have let us go.'

'I doubt it,' assured Brogan.

Clem mounted the horse his sister Emily had been riding and she joined her mother. Brogan took another shirt out of his saddle bag; he had just realised how cold he was.

'Be careful Brogan,' urged Cora. 'If they kill

115

you there ain't no way we can hold out for too long.'

'I hope they do kill him,' spat Clem. 'None of this would've happened but for him. We could've managed.'

'Maybe it wouldn't son,' agreed Brogan. 'But you'd probably all be dead by now. Patterson would've seen to that.'

'He's right Clem,' Cora interrupted her son as he was about to make some remark. 'You gotta learn to trust folk. Whatever you think, your Pa was no good, always drunk, spendin' all our money. He sure gave you a few good beatings for nothin'.'

Clem became solemn. 'I know what my Pa was like. Sure I know he was no good. But he is still my Pa, an' I don't like the idea of no man takin' his place. 'Sides, he wasn't all bad. Me an' him had lots of good times.'

'I know you did Clem,' sighed his mother. 'I didn't make him go, he just packed up an' cleared out one day.'

'That's 'cos you wasn't a proper wife to him,' said Clem. 'Don't give me no bullshit, I know what was goin' on.'

'One day Clem,' said Brogan. 'You'll see it from your Ma's point of view.'

'When I want your preachin' Mister I'll ask for it,' said Clem.

Cora shrugged. Brogan did not give them a chance to say anything else, he turned his horse

116

and rode swiftly off into the darkness. Cora watched sadly for a few minutes, then headed home.

★   ★   ★

The dim outline of the large shed was the only indication that anything existed in the valley as he wound his way through the forest, but other buildings slowly began to emerge from the trees as he got closer. Slade's assertion that there would be no guards proved correct, there was no sign of human life, just two yapping dogs racing alongside his horse, snapping at its feet. Brogan did not mind, he wanted his arrival to be announced, but at first it seemed that nobody was paying any attention to the dogs. He decided that perhaps it was a regular occurrence, this was bear country and he had no doubt that they raided the camp trash heap from time to time.

He left his horse among a clump of trees and deliberately started to goad the dogs, throwing stones at them, but still there was no sign of life. One of the animals became a little bolder, snarling and snapping at his legs. A well aimed boot sent the dog yelping only to return even more savagely. Brogan was ready with his gun.

A door from a nearby cabin creaked slowly open and Brogan could just make out an untidy mop of hair peering round, the barrel of a

117

Winchester wavering about.

'What's goin' on Silas?' another voice called from inside the cabin,

'Can't see nothin',' grunted Silas. 'Must be a bear or somethin' I reckon.'

'Don't usually get bears this time o' year.'

'Somethin' else then,' said Silas. 'Whatever it is, them dogs is sure riled up. In them trees over by the store shed.'

At first the dogs had run over to greet Silas, but quickly returned to yap once again at Brogan.

'Better take a look I reckon,' said the man inside. 'Go wake Craig.'

'No need,' said Silas as another door in the same cabin opened. 'He heard already.'

'What the hell's the matter with them dogs?' demanded Thomas. 'It's three in the morning'.'

'Don't rightly know,' said Silas. 'Somethin' sure got 'em goin'.'

The second man appeared at the door, fully dressed and carrying an oil-lamp. 'Don't sound like no bear, too quiet, it'd be roarin' its head off at them dogs. Don't sound like wolves neither. Dogs wouldn't hang about if it was wolves.'

'Ain't nothin' much left,' said Thomas. ''Ceptin' maybe a man. That's probably it, one of them damned Chinks either makin' a run for it or breakin' into the store. Just like a couple of months ago. Dogs acted the same then.'

The other two looked at each other and grinned. The prospect of a manhunt, even at night, appealed to them. Silas, still in his red flannel Long Johns, reached into the room and tied his gunbelt on, put on his boots and stepped out onto the rather muddy track.

That was as far as he got. A rifle shot echoed round the valley and Silas sprawled lifeless in the mud.

The other two reacted swiftly, diving for cover in the deep shadows. The oil-lamp that had been carried by the other man, Will, crashed down the steps and rolled underneath the cabin.

'You okay Will?' called Thomas.

'Sure,' answered Will. 'Looks like Silas bought it. I can almost touch him. Clean shot through the head.'

'One thing for sure,' muttered Thomas. 'That ain't no Chink out there.'

'Balsam?' queried Will. 'Finally decided to hit back.'

'Don't reckon so,' said Thomas. 'If it was Balsam there'd be more of 'em. This looks like one man, maybe two at most.'

'Who then?' asked Will.

The dogs had achieved the object Brogan had in mind and they were rapidly becoming a nuisance. Brogan did not like killing anything unless he had to, but the dogs were becoming bolder and he was in imminent danger of being attacked by them. Two shots rang out, a slight whimper following each and an eerie silence descended on the valley.

'Who the hell is it?' whispered Thomas, 'An' what does he want?'

'Ask him,' replied Will.

'Hey,' called out Thomas. 'You out there. What's your game?'

'I ain't playin' games Thomas,' called Brogan. 'You remember me? I wouldn't let you kill that boy. Remember?'

'McNally?' shouted Thomas incredulously. 'I heard you'd been whipped. Supposed to be in a pretty bad way.'

'Well I'm here now.'

'What for?' demanded Thomas. 'Ain't nothin' here. Gold was all shipped back to the house yesterday.'

'Ain't gold I'm after.'

'Then what?' called Thomas. 'You sore at me threatenin' to kill you?'

'No. That don't matter. This place belongs to Edmund don't it? That's reason enough.'

The oil-lamp that had rolled under the cabin had started a fire which was now rapidly gaining hold. Will sniffed the air and looked behind him.

'Smoke!' he yelled. 'Cabin's on fire.'

The nearest cover was some twenty yards away and both men suddenly ran for its safety. Brogan chose his target.

The shot had Will crashing headlong into the mud. Thomas almost made it, but fell three or four feet short, groaning in pain. The prostrate body of Will presented an easy target, but Brogan wanted him to reach a horse and ride for help so, apart from a well aimed miss, Brogan allowed the terrified Will to reach the paddock. Not bothering to saddle a horse, he threw himself across its bare back and raced off into the night, clinging to the horse's mane, spurred on by another well aimed miss from Brogan.

Slowly Brogan emerged from the shadows and walked over to Silas who was as Will had said, dead. Thomas was still alive, a wound just below his right shoulder blade. He took the rifles and gunbelts off Thomas and the dead man and threw them to one side.

The wind was fanning the flames of the now fiercely burning cabin toward Thomas, charred timber dropping all around, so he dragged him to the safety of some trees nearby. Quite why he bothered he did not know.

Of course, the entire population of Chinese, some seventy men, women and children, were now wide awake, but not daring to move or make a sound, apart from the uncontrolled crying of a couple of babies. Brogan picked up the guns and walked slowly down the slope to their makeshift huts, calling out as he went.

'Okay you people. You can come out now. Show's over for a while.'

At first nobody took up his offer and he called again. This time the face of an elderly woman showed itself through a crack in one of the doors, her expression a mixture of terror and relief.

'You,' she croaked. 'Why you come back here?'

'Hey, ain't you the mother of the boy I let go?'

'No mother,' cowered the woman coming slowly out of her hut. 'Grandmother. Mother she dead, father also.'

'Well, you can all go now,' grinned Brogan.

'Go?' asked an elderly man coming out of the next hut. 'What you mean. Go?'

'What I said old man,' said Brogan. 'This is your chance to get outa here, find somewhere better.'

'Where we go?' asked the woman. 'We got no place.'

'Any place is better'n this.'

Now most of the others had joined them, all recognising Brogan and jabbering their questions at him, some in English, some in Chinese. The old people, particularly, seemed very bewildered and confused. It was left to the younger men to take charge.

'If we go,' said a young man who appeared to be taking command. 'They will come after us, make us come back.'

'Not when I've finished with 'em,' assured

Brogan. 'Thomas is dyin', maybe dead by now, one of the others is dead. The other one I let go tell Edmund where I am. I want him here an' I don't want you around when he does get here. Now get your things together an' get the hell out of it.' He tossed the rifles and the Colt .45s to the young man. 'Don't know if there's any more about, but these'll help.'

'More guns in store shed,' beamed the young man. 'Bullets too.'

'Then go get 'em, an' anythin' else you need.'

The young man turned to the assembled crowd, silenced them and spoke to them in Chinese. The young were all for leaving, many of the older ones too, but some just stood, unable to appreciate what was happening. Suddenly a group of about twenty raced up to the store shed, breaking down the door and surging through. One by one they emerged carrying almost anything that could be carried. Two of them saw the body of Silas, picked it up and threw it on the fire.

'Where Thomas?' demanded the leader.

Brogan shrugged, even if Thomas was not dead, he guessed that he deserved anything he got. 'Over there,' he pointed. 'In those trees.'

Four of them raced over, shouting triumphantly and firing their guns in the air and found Thomas, still alive. Brogan did not wait to find out what they were going to do to him. He knew he would soon be dead and joining

Silas on the fire.

Eventually the looting mob gathered by the river. Their young leader turned to Brogan. 'I do not know why you do this, or why you helped our friend, but we thank you. At last we are free.'

'What about them in the other camp, an' Balsam's?' asked Brogan.

'We set them free,' announced the young man gleefully. 'We have guns now. Burn down the other camp.'

'An' Balsam's?'

'No, not his. Mister Balsam is a good man. He pay good wages for work. No beat workers. If any of his workers wish to join us they are welcome. Maybe some of us even stay with him.'

'Glad to hear it,' smiled Brogan. 'Now you'd better go. It's a long way.'

The young man turned and ordered everyone to leave, but first the old woman approached Brogan, a gold chain and pendant in her hand which she pressed into his.

'Good luck charm,' she said. 'Please, you take it.'

Brogan did not refuse, he sensed that the woman was giving him the only thing of value she owned, but the life of her grandson and their freedom were of even greater value.

He watched them disappear into the forest and listened to their excited singing dying away.

After about a quarter of an hour all was quiet again.

Out of curiosity he went to where he had left Thomas. What greeted him was not quite what he had expected. A lump of flesh, still with the remnants of clothing on, which he assumed to be the torso, stood upright, impaled on a stake. It had no arms or legs, these lay scattered about, but, most gruesome of all, Thomas's head was also impaled on a stake, staring lifelessly at the fire of the cabin, his genitals protruding from his mouth.

'Hope the poor bastard was dead when they did that,' he muttered.

He threw the limbs on the fire, pulled the torso and head off the stakes and threw them on as well.

★   ★   ★

'Down at the mine?' exclaimed Edmund. 'What the hell's he doin' down there?'

'Settin' fire to everythin' I reckon,' replied Will. 'He killed Craig an' Silas.'

'How about the others, were they with him?'

'What others?' said Will. 'Craig reckoned that there might be two of 'em though. I didn't see none. Didn't see him either come to that. Didn't hang about to find out.'

'You did right Will,' said Slade. 'So, the bastard's wreckin' everythin'.'

125

Will looked about, in his haste he had not really noticed what had happened. He stared at the smouldering remains of the house.

'He hit you too?'

'You might say that,' answered Slade. 'Got away with the Wiesnesky woman an' her kids.' Slade turned to Edmund. 'Boss I don't reckon he took the woman with him. I reckon they gone back to their place, there's only him down there.'

'We'll worry about her later,' roared Edmund. 'Get the men together, all of 'em, includin' Patterson. He can ride.'

'But boss,' pleaded Slade. 'Don't you get it? He's challengin' you, us, all of us; he wants us to go down the mine.'

'Then he's gonna get his wish,' snarled Edmund. 'I want that saddle tramp. How many men we got?'

'Sixteen includin' Patterson, plus you, me an' Will here. That's nineteen.'

'One man against nineteen,' sneered Edmund. 'Not even an idiot like McNally would take them kinda odds. He's hellbent on destruction that's all.'

'He ain't no idiot,' mumbled Slade. 'An' he done a pretty good job of destruction so far.'

'One man against nineteen,' sneered Edmund. 'He may be fast an' good Joe, but he ain't that good.'

'I don't like it,' said Slade. 'Nineteen or not.'

126

'You got the jitters Joe? Ain't never seen you scared of a man before.'

Despite his protestations that they ought to go after Cora Wiesnesky first, Edmund had built up so much hatred of Brogan that all else was secondary. Slade finally gave up trying.

Edmund did not wait for the remaining hour until dawn, he ordered his men to leave immediately.

'What's the matter Slade,' sneered Patterson. 'You scared, wantin' to go after a woman an' kids? This McNally too good for you is he? I heard you pleadin' with Edmund. Pleadin'. You're shit scared.'

'No man calls me scared,' snapped Slade. 'One hand or not, I'll kill you anytime Patterson, if McNally don't do it first.'

'You can try Slade, anytime you like. Or maybe you'd prefer a woman's skirts to hide behind?'

'Cut it out you two,' ordered Edmund, coming between them. 'This ain't the time to be fightin' between ourselves. When we get McNally you can shoot each other to hell as far as I'm concerned, but till then we go together.'

Slade and Patterson stared at each other for a moment or two before Slade finally shrugged and turned away, allowing Patterson a grin of imagined triumph.

Nineteen horses thundered through the gates, leaving the compound completely empty

127

except for Amy Edmund, the fat cook and an elderly housekeeper with no house to keep.

*　　*　　*

Nineteen horses are difficult if not impossible to keep quiet, even if Edmund had wanted to. Brogan detected the approach long before they arrived.

About a mile from the mine, Edmund ordered them to split into three groups. The first group led by himself was to head straight in along the trail. The second group under Jim Patterson moved up the valley side to ride down into the camp. The third group, under Joe Slade, crossed the river and ascended the other side of the valley to come in from the other side. Slade began to wonder if it was one man or an army they were after.

The cabin had now burned itself out, just a few smouldering embers here and there, but, apart from that and the looted store, there was no sign of damage or of Brogan.

Edmund arrived first, leaving the horses among the trees and creeping slowly into the camp. He waved to his men to spread out and search the area.

'Where's the damn Chinks?' he asked Will.

'They were here when I left,' replied Will. 'But it sure looks like they've gone now.'

'Search the huts,' ordered Edmund. 'They

128

can't be far away.'

The men searched every building without success. Slade and Patterson joined him at the same time, each indicating that they had seen nothing.

'He's skipped out,' decided Edmund. 'I knew he wouldn't face us.'

'He ain't skipped out.' A breathless man came running out of the trees behind the store. 'I found his horse. Over there behind the store shed.'

'So, Mister McNally wants to play games does he?' sneered Edmund. 'Okay, spread out again. Find the bastard.'

Their search was interrupted by the rapid approach of a rider from the direction of the other camp, badly injured and almost unable to keep on his horse.

'They wrecked the camp,' he groaned, falling to the ground. 'Burned everythin'. Killed Billy an' Brian. They thought I was dead too.'

'They?' demanded Edmund. 'Who the hell is they?'

'Chinks,' the man gasped. 'Screamin' mob just descended on us, set the others free.'

'Chinks?' said Edmund incredulously. 'You mean the Chinese burned the camp?'

'They had guns,' gasped the man. 'Overran us before we knew what was happenin'. They had guns.' The man gasped his last breath.

'So what do we do now?' asked Slade.

'We find McNally!' roared Edmund. 'That's what.'

Three of the men had ventured into the mine, they never made it out. The roar of dynamite had the rest of them racing toward the mine entrance, choking in the dust billowing out. The entrance was completely blocked by rock which had come down from the roof.

'Three of the boys went in there,' yelled another man. 'They never had a chance.'

'You see anythin'?' demanded Slade.

'No, I was comin' up that bank over there. Saw 'em go in. Explosion happened almost as soon as they was inside. They got buried.'

'Well he ain't in there that's for sure,' said Slade.

Patterson meanwhile had gone to search the sluice shed. A brief shadow flitted across an opening.

'Here,' yelled Patterson. 'He's in here.' He turned to the four men with him. Spread, he's down the bottom end.'

One of them fell groaning as a shot rang out.

'Over there,' hissed one of the others. 'We got him boxed, ain't no way out.'

'Okay McNally,' called Patterson. 'We know you're there. You can't get out. Better give yourself up.' He motioned the other three forward.

The only way through was along a narrow passage. One man reached the passage entrance, fired several shots along it which allowed the others to get close.

'Cover me,' he ordered the others. He ducked and weaved along the passage and crouched at the end by the sluice. After a quick look round he motioned the other two to follow. What they did not see until it was too late was a burning fuse.

'Dynamite!' yelled one, too late.

The explosion met Edmund and Slade as they raced into the shed, ripping along the passage engulfing the three inside in a great billow of flame. The end of the sluice rocked and finally fell apart into the pool of water below. The blast also weakened the supports of the shed which slowly started to cave in.

'Get outa here!' yelled Slade. 'Whole place is comin' down!'

They all ran for the cover of some nearby trees, leaving the injured men pleading with them inside. They watched in awe as the building slowly collapsed, fire spreading through it.

'That's seven men out,' grated Edmund.

'Probably got the whole place rigged up,' said Patterson, joining Edmund and Slade.

'Okay,' said Edmund. 'Spread out. Jim, you take some of the boys over behind the huts. Joe, you take some an' make your way down the track. I'll take the rest of 'em an' go in from this side. We should be able to drive him across the river an' into that rockface. There ain't no way he can get out from there.'

They obediently departed. Patterson and three men reached the huts in safety and slowly started to push forward. As they approached a larger hut, which served as a cookhouse and mess hall, they had to cross open ground. Patterson held back, allowing his three men to go on.

Three quick shots were all that was needed and three men slumped into the dirt.

'Over here Patterson,' came Brogan's mocking voice.

Patterson reeled to look into the barrel of Brogan's rifle as he stepped out of the shadows.

'Still reckon you can take me with your left hand?'

Patterson stared disbelievingly for a brief moment and attempted to raise his gun. He never had a chance to shoot. The roar of the Winchester echoed again in the pale dawn light across the valley and Patterson slumped slowly to the ground, a trickle of blood running down into his sightless eye from the hole in his forehead.

Suddenly it seemed as if all hell had broken loose. Edmund and Slade found themselves pinned down by gunfire from the other side of the river. Brogan grinned. His Chinese friends had come back to help. He decided it was time to get back to Cora.

The Chinese effectively kept the rest pinned down for over an hour before it was noticed that Brogan's horse had gone.

CHAPTER NINE

'His horse 'as gone,' announced Slade. 'Nobody saw him go. I reckon he's gone back to the Wiesnesky woman.'

'Damn him,' cursed Edmund. 'That man's got a charmed life, but I'll get him if it's the last thing I do.'

The shooting had continued since Brogan had left. They had found some bullets in the store shed, but not enough to last. All the men were down to their last few bullets, a couple of them had run out some time ago. The Chinese however, though not skilled in the art of gunfighting, seemed to have a never-ending supply.

'Let's get outa here,' suggested Slade. 'While we still can.'

Despite the exchange of gunfire, it seemed that nobody had been injured on either side. None of the Chinese because they were well hidden and none of Edmund's men because the Chinese were not very accurate.

'We're with you Joe,' agreed most of the men.

Edmund looked at them all with contempt. 'Lettin' a bunch of Chinks get the better of you?'

'Ain't a question of gettin' the better of us,' said Slade. 'We're almost out of bullets. Even a Chink with a gun can kill any of us close to.'

Edmund sighed. They were right of course. 'How many men we got left?'

Slade counted. 'Eight, includin' you an' me.'

'Hell,' muttered Edmund. 'I'd never've believed it. Eleven men taken out. Ain't possible.'

'Plus five from the camps,' reminded Slade. 'I told you boss, we shoulda gone after the Wiesnesky woman first, give us some sorta hold.'

Edmund just grunted and stormed off to his horse as the others followed, talking among themselves. A deathly quiet had descended on the valley as the Chinese realised that their fire was not being returned. They were not foolish enough to press home their advantage, content to sit and see what happened.

The ride back to the remains of the house was slow and silent, Edmund smarting at the disgrace of being driven off by a bunch of Chinese and at being out-manoeuvred by one man.

The numbers that trooped through the gate and their expressions told the whole story. Amy Edmund thought it wise not to ask any

134

questions at the moment.

'We'll get some chow first,' said Edmund. 'Then we go get McNally.'

The men stomped off sullenly to the bunkhouse, while Edmund surveyed the wreckage of his house in daylight. A few smoke-charred brick and stone walls were all that remained, everything else that could burn had been burned.

Amy and the housekeeper had already sifted through the remains in an attempt to salvage what they could, but they found little of any value or importance. Strangely enough, Edmund found that most of the bottles of wine in the cellar, apart from singed labels, had escaped and he started to drown his sorrows in a bottle.

'Bad was it?' Amy asked Slade.

'You might say that,' answered Slade. 'Sixteen men dead all told, an' all the Chinks gone.'

'One man did that?'

'One man,' nodded Slade.

'He's takin' it hard.' She looked across at her husband sat on a smoke-charred wall taking a long drink of wine. 'His own stupid fault though.'

'Got a right to take it hard,' said Slade. 'One mine blocked off, the sluice wrecked an' God knows what damage to the other mine, his house burned down. Maybe the Chinese will be burnin' the rest by now.'

'I know,' sighed Amy. 'Believe me, I've been just as hard hit, but none of this need ever have happened if he'd not got it into his head to make McNally work for him. Should've killed him at the start.'

'You hard hit,' scorned Slade. 'Sure you lost your home, all your pretty dresses, but that's all. He can rebuild, so can you. There's enough gold in the strongroom to buy an' sell most men.'

'Guess so,' agreed Amy. She gave Slade a long sideways look. 'Ever thought of stealin' it?'

'Man would be a fool not to have thought about it,' admitted Slade. 'I know I have, an' most of the boys from time to time.'

'That's all though,' prompted Amy. 'Just thought about it?'

'That's all.'

'So have I,' said Amy. 'Phil an' me, we got nothin' in common, 'ceptin' maybe a taste for the good life. I get most everythin' I want out here, but I miss the city. All them fancy stores, restaurants an' most of all rubbin' shoulders with State Governors, even the President sometimes.'

Slade gave Amy a long hard look. 'Just what you gettin' at?'

'He's finished here,' said Amy. 'Even if he does get McNally, his workers are gone. He ain't gonna get others too easy, an' he's long past grubbin' about for his own gold. I want out while there's still enough left for the takin'.'

'An' you want me to help you?'

'Go with me Joe,' she grasped his arm. 'We could be rich. There's more'n enough gold in the strongroom. We could have a good time together.'

Slade took another long hard look at her. 'I'm no fool,' he said eventually. 'Sure, we could probably get the gold, but you'd soon get fed up with me. Then you'd be schemin' how to get rid of me an' get my share.'

A faint smile played on her lips. 'No Joe,' she snuggled closer. 'I've always admired you; never shown it of course, but I have.'

Slade pushed her away. Even now he did not intend to get on the wrong side of Edmund.

'He ain't no fool either,' he said. 'He's got plenty in the bank, he'll survive an' he ain't a very forgivin' man. He'll hunt us down as sure as anythin'.'

'Then kill him,' she urged. 'As his wife, I would inherit everythin'.'

'You make it sound too easy,' said Slade.

'It is easy Joe.'

'An' just how am I supposed to kill him?'

'Go after McNally,' she smiled. 'People do get killed in gunfights.'

'You're suggestin' I shoot him an' blame it on McNally?'

'Right Joe,' she snuggled closer again.

137

'Couldn't be easier.'

A grunt from Edmund made them part. He came over eyeing them curiously and sat down between them.

'Gettin' mighty close you two.'

'Just talkin',' said Amy. 'Wonderin' what to do about McNally.'

'Only one thing to do with him,' grunted Edmund again. 'Kill the bastard.'

'Just how?' asked Slade. 'He done a pretty good job of avoidin' us so far.'

'He'll be at Cora Wiesnesky's place,' said Edmund. 'This time he'll be boxed in. No trees. Open ground all round. Sure, he can hold out a while, but not forever. We got plenty of ammunition. We can afford to sit an' wait.'

'Guess so,' agreed Slade. 'Then what?'

'What you mean? Then what?'

'What about the mines? How you gonna reopen 'em without no labour? Ain't nobody gonna work for you like them Chinks did.'

'We'll manage,' said Edmund.

'We?' asked Amy.

'Yeh,' replied Edmund. 'You, me, Joe an' the boys that's left.'

'Me an' the boys ain't labourers,' pointed out Slade. 'Never have been, never will be. They ain't prepared to grub in the dirt for a livin'.'

'An' you?' asked Edmund.

'I might,' said Slade. 'As an equal partner.'

Edmund thought about it for a few minutes.

'Okay Joe. You got yourself a deal. All you gotta do now is talk the others into it. They'll get paid of course.'

Amy glanced at Slade in alarm. She had not expected her husband to agree to such a thing, and the prospect of hard work did not appeal.

'I'll try,' said Slade. 'But I ain't promisin' nothin'.' He stood up and dusted himself off and went over to the bunkhouse.

The six men were huddled in a corner, obviously in deep conversation about something which suddenly stopped as Slade came in. An uncomfortable silence fell upon the room. Slade knew that he was going to have a difficult task on his hands. He sat amongst them, looked at each in turn and explained what Edmund wanted.

'We ain't miners Joe,' said one. ''Ceptin' maybe Will here. Seems like too much hard work for practically nothin'.'

'What else you got?' asked Slade.

'We'll survive,' said Will. 'We all got prices on our heads somewhere. We can get by, takin' what we want. Besides, we already got plans.'

'Plans?' asked Slade. 'What plans?'

'You can be in if you want to Joe,' said one of the others. 'We'll even take orders from you. You got brains Joe. None of us is much good when it comes to thinkin'. We could use you.'

'I got plans too,' smiled Slade. 'Unfortunately it don't include any of you.'

'Suit yourself,' grunted Will. 'We can manage without you.'

The door crashed open and Edmund burst in. 'Well?' he demanded.

'Well, nothin' Edmund,' sneered Will, standing up.

'I want you out after that bum McNally, now,' roared Edmund. 'An' it's "Boss" or "Mister Edmund" to you.'

'Okay, MISTER Edmund,' grinned Will. 'We ain't fightin' no more battles for you. You're on your own, unless Joe here sticks with you.'

'Shit scared of McNally, a no-good saddle bum, are you?'

'Saddle bum he may be,' said one. 'No good? You got it wrong MISTER Edmund. He's good, very good, an' yes, we're scared of him; he done a damned good job so far. We don't intend joinin' the others bein' shot or blown to pieces.'

'We're leavin',' said Will. 'An' since Joe seems to have other plans, I guess we got no alternative.' He whipped out his gun and levelled it at Edmund, who gazed at it in amazement. At the same time two of the others covered Slade. 'We ain't leavin' empty-handed though,' he grinned. 'Keys Edmund. Keys to the strongroom. We're takin' as much gold as we can carry.'

'That's my gold!' screamed Edmund. 'Nobody takes my gold!'

'We are,' laughed one. 'We earned that gold,

now we're gonna take it.'

Slade made no attempt to stop them. He could not blame them, maybe he should have joined them. Suddenly, Edmund lunged at Will, but he was ready. Raising his gun, he brought it crashing down on the back of Edmund's head. Edmund groaned and slumped across a bunk.

'You had your chance Joe,' said Will. 'Now it's too late. Search him.' He nodded to Edmund.

One of them rifled through Edmund's pockets, finding a wad of ten-dollar bills, a gold watch and chain and finally the keys to the strongroom.

'Don't try to stop us Joe,' warned Will. 'I'll kill you. I ain't so fancy with a gun as you, but I can shoot straight.'

'Don't intend to try,' assured Slade. 'I still got plans of my own.'

'I can guess,' said Will. 'An' I reckon your plans include Amy.' Slade nodded. 'I'll leave it to you to kill Edmund then. Good luck Joe.'

They left the bunkhouse and headed to the strongroom, the solidly locked building on the side of the wall, eventually finding the right keys and whooping with joy as they threw themselves in. Slade walked slowly back to Amy.

'Seems they is quittin',' he smiled.

'With our gold?' exclaimed Amy. 'They can't

do that.'

'They can an' they are,' said Slade.

'No they're not,' spat Amy, grabbing a rifle and racing to the strongroom, Slade following, smiling to himself.

She waited patiently, the gun hidden behind her, while the six men staggered out with bags of gold and tied them to their horses. Eventually, having decided they could carry no more, they started to mount up.

'About a hundred thousand dollars' worth,' beamed Will. 'That should see us through for a while. You can have the rest.'

'We'll take it all,' grated Amy, suddenly producing the rifle and firing very accurately from her waist. Will groaned slightly and crashed lifelessly off his horse. The gun spat again, this time accompanied by the crack of Slade's Colt .45. Two more men fell. The other three tried to make a run for it, but only made a few yards before they too crashed to the ground, a bag of gold spilling out onto the dirt.

Two men were still alive, but Amy was ruthless, a side of her which Slade had never seen before. She stood over the injured men and shot each through the head.

'Remind me never to trust you with a gun,' he said, taking the rifle off her.

'I can shoot,' she said. 'Just 'cos I'm a woman don't mean I don't know how to.'

A sound from the bunkhouse made them

turn; Edmund was staggering toward them. 'You stopped 'em!' he cried then, seeing the gold in the dust, sank to his knees and scooped it up lovingly.

'We stopped 'em,' sneered Amy. 'More'n you could do.'

'I won't forget this,' promised Edmund.

Amy nodded at Slade and at the grovelling body of her husband. 'Now,' she whispered.

'No,' whispered Slade shaking his head. 'Better like you said.'

'What about this McNally?' prompted Amy.

'McNally,' hissed Edmund. 'Yes, McNally. Come on Joe, we got work to do.'

Slade glanced at Amy and winked. 'Okay, partner.'

*   *   *

Brogan had ridden hard back to Cora, and was somewhat embarrassed when she raced forward and threw her arms round his neck, laughing and crying at the same time. He gently pushed her away.

'Thank God you're back safe,' she sobbed.

'Ain't got too much time,' he said. 'They'll realise I've gone before long an' come after me.'

'You ran from 'em,' sneered Clem. 'Just like I figured. Yeller livered.'

Brogan suddenly exploded. 'First thing I'm gonna do is teach you some manners boy.' He

143

dropped his gunbelt and took off his leather trouser belt, wrapping the buckle end round his hand.

Clem backed away nervously. He had suffered many beltings at the hand of his father and was still terrified of them. Brogan grabbed hold of him by the shirt, held him at arms length and proceeded to lash the belt across the boy's buttocks. Cora did not try to interfere, she was almost pleased that someone had taken her son to task.

At length Brogan allowed Clem to sink to the ground sobbing and stroking his tender rear end. 'I did not run from 'em boy. I must've killed about ten of 'em, but there was too many to handle. The Chinese is keepin' 'em occupied for the time bein'.'

'Last Post' had witnessed the beating and was sniggering to himself. ''Bout time that young brat was put in his place.'

'I got a job for you soldier,' said Brogan. 'A scoutin' job, just like in the Army.'

'Yes sir,' said 'Last Post' snapping to attention. 'Best scout the Army ever had.'

'I'm sure you were,' grinned Brogan. 'Okay now soldier. I want you to ride out to that ridge over there an' keep a lookout for Edmund an' his men. If you see 'em, ride hard back here an' report. Got that?'

'Yes sir,' said 'Last Post' still stiffly at attention. 'Permission to take my old buffalo rifle along sir?'

'Permission granted,' agreed Brogan.

'Last Post' beamed, went into the house and returned a few minutes later dressed in cavalry uniform, clutching his huge rifle.

'Never knew he had that,' said Cora. 'But then I never looked in that old box of his.'

The uniform was a little overlarge since he had lost a lot of weight since his Army days. He proudly thrust his arm forward to display the insignia of sergeant.

Brogan grinned. 'Go to it sergeant, everythin' depends on you.'

'Yes sir,' barked 'Last Post'. 'You can count on me sir.' He marched off stiffly and eventually led one of the horses out of the barn, managing to struggle into the saddle. He rode over to Brogan and Cora, saluted stiffly, waited for Brogan to return the salute and then rode off.

'I guess he's happy,' said Cora. 'Was it really necessary to send him off?'

'Yes,' said Brogan. 'It's as well to know just when they're comin'.'

'How many?'

'Nine, maybe ten,' said Brogan.

'That's a lot of guns to deal with.'

'There's three of us, four if you include 'Last Post'. The boy reckons he can use a rifle, this'll be his chance to prove it.'

'You don't have to worry about me Mister,'

scowled Clem. 'I can use one.'

'I hope I don't have to worry about you,' smiled Brogan. 'Unless you want your ass tannin' again.'

Brogan moved to the top of a small hill to look for 'Last Post' when he rode in. A few minutes later he was joined by Cora. For some considerable time they sat in silence, gazing across the barren landscape, both knowing what was going through each other's minds.

'You have made your mind up haven't you?' said Cora.

'Never really had one to make up,' said Brogan. 'Wouldn't work Cora, an' you know it.'

'How d'you know if you don't try?'

'I just know,' said Brogan. 'I don't belong tied to no woman or no land. The whole world is my land.'

'An' all the women in it?'

'Maybe,' smiled Brogan. 'Ain't never really thought about that.'

'Guess I can tell Clem you ain't stoppin' then,' sighed Cora. 'That should make him happy.'

'Guess so.'

'Boy like that needs a man around,' said Cora. 'Keep him in order like you just did. Talk man talk, things like that.'

'Hell Cora,' said Brogan. 'I know nothin' about kids. Been so long ago since I was one, I clean forgot how.'

'I ain't gonna try pleadin' with you Brogan,' said Cora. 'You know what I want, but you got a right to decide for yourself I guess.'

'It's for the best,' assured Brogan. 'Man like me, driftin' all his life, can't settle down. I'd be worse'n a bear with a sore head in a few weeks.'

Cora shrugged and returned to the house in tears. Her children met her at the door, Clem now more subdued.

'He ain't stoppin' then Ma?' asked Clem.

'No, he don't want to,' she choked. 'Says it wouldn't work.'

'On account of me?' asked Clem.

'No son,' she assured. 'Ain't nothin' to do with you at all.'

Clem went to join Brogan. 'You ain't sore at Ma on account of me are you?'

'I ain't sore at your Ma,' smiled Brogan. 'An' I ain't sore at you either boy. It's just the way things are. Me stoppin' would only lead to trouble in the end.'

'I reckon I'd kinda like havin' a grown man about the place,' said Clem. 'I know I been pigheaded. Jealous I guess.'

'Ain't your fault son,' assured Brogan. 'Sorry about the jaw an' the tannin' just now.'

'Guess I deserved both,' grinned Clem.

The two sat in silence on the hill top for over two hours, Brogan beginning to think that Edmund was not going to come. Then, faintly

147

on the breeze he heard something. He usually
heard everything.

'Listen Clem,' he whispered. 'Hear that?'

Clem strained his ears. 'No, can't hear
nothin'.'

Brogan listened again. 'There it is again.
Bugle call. "Last Post", he can't make it back,
he's playin his bugle to warn us.'

'Still can't hear nothin'.' said Clem. 'But I'll
take your word on it. What do we do now?'

'In the house,' said Brogan. 'Get all the guns
an' ammunition you got, get by a window an'
keep down. Your Ma too. Girls'd be safer in
your bunk, covered with blankets an' things.
Go on, you're the man of the house, go tell
'em.'

'Yes sir,' grinned Clem. 'An' thanks Brogan.'

'My pleasure Clem.'

'What you gonna do?'

'Wait here a while. Should be able to get back
easy enough.'

Clem departed and took charge of
arrangements in the house. Brogan waited.

'What the hell's goin' on?' he muttered to
himself. 'One rider?'

A solitary horse and rider headed slowly over
the rough heathland, not appearing to be in too
much of a hurry. Slowly the shape came into
focus as being Joe Slade. Brogan scanned the
surrounding countryside for signs of the others,
but did not see any.

Distance can be deceptive and it seemed that Slade was never going to reach the hill Brogan was sitting on. He did not know if Slade had seen him or not, he certainly had not moved, and at a distance would have looked like a rock or a bush. It seemed Slade had not seen him.

Leaving his horse at the base of the hill, not even glancing up, Slade crept slowly down toward the house. He eventually took position and seemed content to wait. Brogan surveyed the surrounding land again and waited some time before descending on Slade.

'Don't even think about goin' for your gun,' ordered Brogan. 'Drop 'em well away.'

'Might've known I wouldn't catch you out Brogan,' said Slade, obediently casting his rifle to one side and unbuckling his belt.

'I don't get it Slade,' said Brogan. 'You come all the way out here by yourself to get me?'

'Sure looks like it don't it?' said Slade. 'I figured if nineteen of us couldn't get you, maybe just one man could.'

'Looks like you got it wrong again,' said Brogan. Something was wrong. It had been too easy. 'Where's the rest of 'em?'

Slade laughed. 'Rest of 'em?' He laughed again. 'Dead Brogan, all dead 'ceptin' me an' Edmund.'

'I didn't kill 'em all,' said Brogan. 'I made it nine, maybe ten.'

'Eleven actually,' corrected Slade.

'There was nineteen of you. What happened to the others? Chinese better with guns than you expected?'

'Hell no,' said Slade. 'Couldn't hit a barn door at five paces.'

'What then?'

'You ain't gonna believe this,' laughed Slade again. 'But me an' Amy Edmund, we killed the others,' he went on to explain.

'Maybe you shoulda taken up with 'em,' said Brogan. 'Amy Edmund ain't your type, or you hers, an' you know it.'

'I know it,' agreed Slade. 'I been thinkin' about that on the way over here. I finally decided to take all the gold myself.'

'Okay. So what about Edmund?'

'He gets himself killed.'

'An' I'm supposed to be the one that does it?'

'That's what it's supposed to look like,' agreed Slade.

'I don't get it,' said Brogan. 'So where the hell is Edmund?'

'Right behind you McNally,' came Edmund's voice. 'Glad I heard all that Slade. I kinda figured somethin' was goin' on.'

'What the hell you doin' here' said Slade. 'You was supposed to come in from behind the house.'

'So you could shoot me?' said Edmund. 'I heard that old fool givin' the signal on his bugle, so I doubled back an' came up the valley.

150

Now I kill you both.'

'Get on with it Edmund,' said Brogan.

'First I want you to suffer McNally,' gloated Edmund. 'Slade too. Drop your gun.'

'No chance Edmund,' said Brogan. 'Since you're gonna kill me anyway. I'm gonna die tryin'.'

'Have it your way McNally,' rasped Edmund. 'I'd wanted to watch you suffer, but I guess this'll have to do.'

There was no need for Brogan to do anything. A deafening roar filled the air. For a brief moment Edmund hung like a rag doll, blood spraying over nearby rocks as the charge from the buffalo rifle ripped through his back. As the echo died away, 'Last Post' appeared and saluted Brogan.

'All the enemy accounted for sir.'

'Well done sergeant,' said Brogan returning the salute.

'Messy but effective,' grinned Slade.

'Very,' agreed Brogan. 'Okay, so what about you now? You wanna test your luck against me?'

'If you don't mind Brogan,' sighed Slade. 'That's one pleasure I'll give up on. Maybe some other time. Not that I'm scared of you mind, just don't seem much point to it any more.' He picked up his guns and scrambled back up the slope to face the reloaded buffalo gun.

'Hold it sergeant,' ordered Brogan. 'War's over.'

'Yes sir,' responded 'Last Post' obediently. 'We takin' him prisoner sir?'

'No sergeant,' smiled Brogan. 'This one we let go. He can take Edmund's body back to Amy. Might as well leave her somethin'.'

'She'll get all his money in the bank. The gold'll do me. Man can do a lot with that kinda money.'

'What the hell's goin' on?' demanded Cora.

'I'll explain later,' said Brogan. 'In the meantime Joe here is on his way with Edmund's body.'

CHAPTER TEN

'Just passin' through?' asked the storekeeper absently. 'Most is just passin' through Maneheim.' He looked up. 'You. Maybe this time you'd better just keep goin'. Lost most my trade on account of you.'

'Cora Wiesnesky will probably make some of that up,' grinned Brogan. 'Found a rich deposit on her land. She's lookin' for hired help.'

'I hear Balsam's got more'n he can handle.'

'I heard,' said Brogan. 'I already sent a message to 'em.' He left the store and went to the saloon. There was only one bargirl.

152

'Other one went harin' after Slade,' explained Fat Pete. 'Reckons he owes her, 'specially since we heard he suddenly become rich.'

'Hear anythin' of Amy Edmund?'

'Packed up. Gone to California somewhere to sort out Edmund's money. Two mines empty now. Got to lie unused for one year without anyone layin' claim to 'em before they can be reopened. Was thinkin' about settin' up myself.'

'Stick to bartenderin',' said Brogan. 'Lot less trouble.'

Photoset, printed and bound in Great Britain by REDWOOD PRESS LIMITED, Melksham, Wiltshire